Contents

The Horror Handbook

1
The Art of Horror

Let's not beat about the bush: you bought this book, or you borrowed or stole it, because you like horror stories. There is nothing wrong with that. You are not the only one who enjoys getting the creeps. Throughout the ages people have told each other horror stories. It seems we can't do without them. By the way, if you *have* stolen this book, you must return it at once. Because if you don't, one night, when you least expect it, an old friend of mine – a big, nasty werewolf – will come and get you.

If you look up "horror" in the *Oxford English Dictionary*, it will tell you it means: "An intense feeling of fear, shock, or disgust."

It fails to mention that horror can be fun, for instance when you read a horror book or watch a horror film. What is so great about it is that you can enjoy the horror in your bed or in a chair, where you know you are safe. You know it is all made up. And if it gets too scary, you just look away, or you shut the book and stick your head under the blanket. The worst that can happen is that you have a nightmare, but that is a price worth paying for a good horror story. And of course the next day you will pick up the book again, because you want to know what happens next.

Horror is an art. Really. Just think of 'The Boy Who Went Forth to Learn Fear', a folk tale told by the brothers Grimm in the nineteenth century. The main character in the story is a boy who is a bit thick. He doesn't get the art of horror and sets out to discover what it is to shiver with fear. But even after three nights in a haunted castle, he still has not mastered the art of horror. Eventually he marries a princess. She is fed up with his moaning about not being able to shiver with fear, so one night she empties a bucketful of cold water with little fish in it over his head. He wakes up and cries out, "But, my dear wife, what is that? I am shivering, I am shivering! At last I know what it is to shiver with fear." And he was pleased as Punch.

You see, horror is an art. What is more, it is clear that you are not stupid if you know how to shiver with fear.

One of the main things about horror stories is that stuff happens that can't happen in real life. Dead people come out of their graves and cut-off hands come alive. You could call it an "alternative reality". A reality where anything is possible. People who don't like horror stories don't know what they are missing.

Take vampires, werewolves, witches, ghosts, monsters and zombies, for example. People have been telling stories about them for centuries. In this book you will find information about where they come from, what they look like, how they behave, how to fight them and so forth. All the creeps we will discuss are actually related. This *Horror Handbook* is like a family portrait. Without this family of creeps, life (and books) would be a lot more boring, even if everyone knows it is all made up.

You see, the art of horror is to pretend for a little while that it is all true. By using your imagination you can make a horror story as scary as you want. For those

5

without imagination, a soft knock at the door is just that: a soft knock at the door. But for those who master the art of horror, a soft knock means something very different. Who or what is behind that door? A vampire? An eight-armed monster? A man with an iron hook? The dentist? A horror fan won't go to sleep until he or she knows where that soft knock came from. Those who don't understand the art of horror will calmly climb into their beds and close their eyes. They are not afraid of anything. But one night, when they are asleep and least expect it, one of these monsters might come for them...

In this *Horror Handbook* you will find a description of all these creeps. Sometimes the way they behave or look is very similar. And they all share at least one thing: people write about them to give us the shivers.

You will see that you can split the horror family into two groups. There are creeps that are entirely made up, like vampires and werewolves. And there are creeps that actually exist or have existed, such as witches and zombies. As for ghosts, we don't know for sure if they really exist or not. Some people see them, but most have never laid eyes on one. You can make up your own mind as to whether you believe in them.

Apart from being a book where you can look things up, this *Horror Handbook* can come in handy when you are under threat.

If you notice for example that your teacher's chest hair starts to poke above his shirt collar, and if he has a monobrow to boot, it may be a good idea to calmly read the chapter on werewolves.

If your teacher has been looking very pale of late, and you have the impression that her canine teeth are getting pointier, I advise you to start right away on the chapter on vampires. Perhaps it is not too late.

I would like to thank Eddy C. Bertin, who wrote Chapter 8 about horror films. The number of horror films in existence is unbelievably huge. Many of them have little to do with the fun side of horror. They are gruesome and gory horror films, and that is not what this book is about. That is why we don't discuss films that have murderers with chainsaws and other idiots in them, or where arms and legs are ripped off just for laughs, or where buckets full of blood are splattered all across the screen.

In the last chapter three classic horror books will be discussed. They were actually written for adults, but because they really are the forerunners of the modern horror story, we felt we had to include them in this *Horror Handbook*. My thanks go to Jack Didden, who researched these horror classics and wrote the chapter.

To finish off: please enjoy that creepy feeling, but don't forget to look under your bed before you switch off the light. You never know.

2
Vampires

His eyes flamed red with devilish passion; the great nostrils of the white aquiline nose opened wide and quivered at the edge; and the white sharp teeth, behind the full lips of the blood-dripping mouth, clamped together like those of a wild beast.
- From *Dracula*, by Bram Stoker.

Vampires are possibly the most beloved and also the most feared of all monsters. People have been telling stories about them for centuries. Virtually everyone has heard of vampires.

But what *is* a vampire? Vampires are creatures that are neither dead nor alive. They are also immortal. That is all rather curious if you think about it. But those who have mastered the art of horror know that we are dealing with an "alternative reality" where anything is possible.

Vampires are called the undead, because they are neither dead nor alive. Both men and women can be vampires. The word "vampire" is derived from a

Eastern European word that means "undead". It was first used in English in 1734.

What do vampires do?

During the day, vampires sleep in the coffin in which they were buried. They come out at night looking for blood. That is what they live on. They don't eat or drink anything else. Vampires *love* the blood of living humans. Male vampires prefer to bite women, while female vampires would rather have a man's neck to sip blood from. Only if they can't find any humans, they make do with a chicken or a sheep. Once they have found their victim, they sink their long, sharp fangs into their neck. After that, they drink the blood straight from the artery.

These undead creatures are blood-sucking monsters, then. They usually visit the same victim more than once, until they have drunk all their blood. Then the victim turns into a vampire too, and starts looking for new victims to bite. If no one did anything about them, their numbers would grow in no time. Fortunately there are a few effective ways of killing vampires.

What does a vampire look like?

Old-fashioned vampires. In most old stories vampires are dressed in black and wear long black capes. They never once put on something a bit more colourful. The same goes for female vampires. Because of their black clothes, they can easily disappear into the shadows and move about at night as good as undetected. This vampire outfit is in fact very old-fashioned and dates back to the nineteenth century, when Bram Stoker's book *Dracula* was published. You could also recognize these "old" vampires by their nails, which were incredibly long. Sometimes they also had hair growing on the palms of their hands.

Modern vampires. Modern vampires wear all sorts of clothes and accessories. Skinny jeans, high tops, bandanas, black tie, sunglasses, nose rings, depending on what they were wearing the moment they became vampires. Modern vampires also have various hairstyles, ranging from a shock of hair dyed in three colours to a ponytail or  no hair at all. It is all possible. Modern vampires are more aware of fashion than old ones. Sometimes they decide to wear something different from the good old black cape. In the 1988 film *The Lost Boys*, young punk vampires race through town on their motorbikes dressed in long, black leather coats.

Other vampires. The vampires discussed above are common in stories from Western Europe and America. But in other countries, vampires can be very different. In Chinese stories there are vampires that have green hair on their entire body and even give off light. In Bulgaria they believe that vampires only have one nostril. In Japanese stories there are vampires that look like huge cats. The Pelesit, a Malaysian vampire, has the shape of a cricket with a pointy tail, which it uses to pierce people's skins.

Fangs. The most important weapon vampires have, both the old and the new ones, is their razor-sharp fangs. With them they make tiny holes in their victims' necks, allowing them to drink blood straight from their arteries. All you need to see on the cover of a book or on a billboard announcing a film is two fangs, and you know it will be about vampires. They are the vampire's symbol.

Deathly pale faces. Vampires have deathly pale faces. The reason for this is a lack of blood and sunshine. This is no wonder, because vampires never come out into the sun. They can't bear daylight. Before the sun rises, vampires crawl off somewhere dark, usually their coffin. If they didn't, they would turn into a heap of ash. Even one ray of sunshine will scorch their skin. Only when they have had their fill of blood can you see their pale cheeks flush. Even their eyes turn blood-red.

Protection against daylight

Modern vampires dare to go out more and more. They use sunglasses, coloured contact lenses, gloves, hats and sunscreen with a high protection factor.

Hiding places

Vampires love to hang out in graveyards. They feel at home among the dead, because they are themselves somewhere between dead and alive – and there are plenty of places to hide. In the old days, tombs were often like little houses where the coffins of an entire family were kept. More than one vampire could therefore hide in one of these tombs. But given the choice, vampires prefer their own coffins.

They carry them around wherever they go. On the inside, a vampire's coffin is filthy and splattered with blood, because his mouth is often one bloody mess when he lies down. When he has been too greedy and had too much to drink, the blood just oozes out of his mouth while he sleeps. Vampires also keep a bit of earth from the place they were born in their coffin. This gives them strength.

Vampires never stay in the same place very long. They are afraid they will be caught, which is why they travel around looking for new victims and somewhere safe to hide. If they have enough money, they rent a room or a house and put their coffin in the bedroom. In the old days they used to drag their coffins around with them as they travelled in horse-drawn coaches, and on trains and ships. Nowadays they just use DHL and have their coffins delivered wherever they go.

In a book I wrote in 1990, *Vampire in the School*, a vampire hides his coffin in a large wooden chest in the headmaster's office.

Vampires who don't have a coffin of their own – because they became vampires before they were buried, for example – hide in other dark places like basements, warehouses, abandoned factories, the Underground and so forth. We could, in fact, be surrounded by vampires without having the slightest idea.

Travelling vampires

Needless to say, vampires usually travel by night. Still, sometimes travelling can be a real pain.

For some obscure reason they can't cross flowing water by themselves. They need the help of others, often criminals or people who would do anything for money without asking too many questions. In the old days, they let themselves be carried across rivers and oceans in their coffins. Nowadays they have it much, much easier because of aeroplanes. A vampire just books an overnight flight. He travels first class, while his coffin is in the hold with the other luggage, perhaps a large crate that says "bananas" or "whisky". And no one is the wiser.

How old do vampires get?

Time has no meaning to a vampire. When someone becomes a vampire because they were bitten several times, he or she will look the same from then on. Nothing ever changes. A three-thousand-year-old vampire can look like a baby or a ten-year-old, depending on when they were bitten.

Vampires don't grow older, but according to some they look younger when they have had some blood to drink. For a little while they become fresh and young again. Maybe that is why they love blood so much.

With a bit of luck, a vampire can grow to be thousands or tens of thousands of years old. If they don't get killed by a vampire hunter, that is.

No reflection or shadow

Vampires don't have a reflection. Maybe that is just as well. If they saw their own faces, with those long fangs, they would be scared to death. You will never find a mirror in a vampire's house. They hate them. You should be very suspicious of people who don't have mirrors in their house.

Generally speaking, vampires don't have a shadow either. Film vampires are an exception – but then again, they are played by actors.

Shape-shifting

When vampires are found out, they can change into a bat in a split second and escape. If they want to, they can change themselves into a dog or

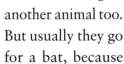

another animal too. But usually they go for a bat, because that way they can disappear quickly into the night and cover large distances on the wing.

Power over animals and the weather

There are a number of animals that vampires control: wolves, rats, dogs, bats and flies. They follow the vampires' orders.

Vampires use them to protect themselves, to pass on messages or to lure their victims into a trap. Vampires can also influence the weather. They can make fog appear, for example. As a result, people get lost in the fog and the vampires' wolves or dogs drive the victim straight into their masters' open mouths.

Invitation

Vampires can't enter someone's house unless they have been invited in by one of the people who live there. Once they have been invited in, they can come and go as they please. The trick many vampires use, naturally, is to disguise themselves and get permission to enter. So be wary of inviting strangers into your house on foggy evenings! Before you know it, they will sink their fangs into your neck and come back every night after that. No doors or windows can stop them then. A vampire can change not only into an animal, but also into a wisp of mist. That way they enter your house through cracks and crannies. Once inside, they change back into a vampire.

Hypnosis

Never look a vampire in the eye, or you will be finished. You will be like putty in their hands, and before you know it, you will be bitten. Vampires can easily hypnotize their victims. When a person has been bitten, they won't remember a thing the next day. They will start to look paler and paler and lose weight. They will stay out of the sun without knowing why. Only when they have become a vampire themselves will they understand. But by then it is too late.

Strength

Vampires are incredibly strong. They are as strong as ten men put together, and when they have just guzzled up their fill of blood, their strength doubles. Because they are so strong, they are almost impossible to beat. That is why the best time to attack a vampire is during the day when they are asleep. But be careful: even when they sleep they can open their eyes and grab hold of you with their hypnotic eyes until it gets dark!

How do you become a vampire?

There are a few ways you can become a vampire. No one becomes a vampire of his own free will.

A vampire's bite. You can become a vampire because you have been bitten by one. Usually you need to be bitten more than once. The vampire must bite his or her victim a number of times and drink all their blood until they die. When they are dead, they become vampires too. When someone is about to become a vampire, the only way they won't end up being one is if the vampire is killed. Victims of vampires quickly develop anaemia. You can recognize them by their pale faces.

Drinking a vampire's blood. You can also change into a vampire if you drink a vampire's blood. Vampires can pierce their wrist with their fangs or scratch their chest with their nails and force their victim to drink blood from the wound. From that moment on, a change will come over the victim, because he or she now has vampire blood running through their veins. They will become slaves of the vampire whose blood they drank, and will be sent on errands all the time to fetch "tasty morsels" for their master.

This is how it usually happens, but some people are destined from birth to become vampires.

Born with teeth. This is the case for babies who are born with teeth. In Eastern European countries, parents are decidedly dischuffed when this happens.

For starters, it is painful to breast-feed such babies. But the worst thing is that when they die, they will become vampires. If they die very young, you will end up with a baby vampire.

The seventh child. The seventh child born of the same parents is also likely to reach vampirehood after it dies. Fortunately, families tend to be smaller these days and the chance of having seventh-child vampires is therefore much smaller too.

Christmas. If you're born on Christmas Day, or just before or after, you are very likely to become a vampire later in life. Not such a merry Christmas for you, then.

Born with the caul. If you are born "with the caul" – a thin kind of skin that sometimes covers your head at birth – you run the risk of becoming a vampire when you die. They also say that people who are born with the caul have psychic powers. So you might end up becoming a psychic vampire.

Suicide. In Transylvania (a region in Romania), they believe that someone who kills himself will change into a vampire.

If one of these five things applies to you, chances are that you will end up joining the vampire club. But if you were born on a Saturday, there is hope. People who are born on a Saturday can never become vampires. That is why they make excellent vampire hunters, since they don't run any risks.

How to fight vampires

How can you prevent this club of vampires from spreading day after day until the whole world population has become a vampire? Because that is what would happen if there were no ways of killing vampires. And how can you protect yourself against the attack of a vampire? These are important questions for the horror fans who want to enjoy their art as long as they can, but preferably not for ever and ever.

Vampire hunters. When a vampire has been spotted in town, go on Google and search for your nearest "vampire hunter".

Vampire hunters are people who make a living out of terminating vampires. They usually work alone, but sometimes they join forces. In my book *Vampire in the School* a group of elderly vampire hunters have formed the UFVK (Union for Fearless Vampire Killers).

A few things are absolutely essential for any vampire hunter. You can 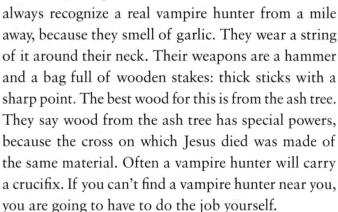 always recognize a real vampire hunter from a mile away, because they smell of garlic. They wear a string of it around their neck. Their weapons are a hammer and a bag full of wooden stakes: thick sticks with a sharp point. The best wood for this is from the ash tree. They say wood from the ash tree has special powers, because the cross on which Jesus died was made of the same material. Often a vampire hunter will carry a crucifix. If you can't find a vampire hunter near you, you are going to have to do the job yourself.

A wooden stake. The safest way to get rid of a vampire is to find one while he is asleep in a coffin during the day. First you must find the coffin of course. Graveyards, the Underground, basements and abandoned factories are the best places to look. Traces of blood may point you in the right direction. Once you have found the coffin, check if it is still light outside. If not, you could be in for a nasty surprise, because as soon as the sun sets, the vampire wakes up, and you will be lost. If necessary, put off your task until the next morning.

The vampire you are looking for will be lying still in his coffin, sleeping quietly, but without breathing and sometimes with his eyes wide open. Remember never to look him in the eye! Take your hammer, ram the pointy end of the stake right through his heart and nail the vampire to the bottom of the coffin. The moment you pierce a vampire with a stake, he will open his eyes and let out a chilling shriek. You must prepare yourself for that – if not, it will scare you out of your wits. Some blood will probably squirt out of the wound. And if the vampire has had a lot to drink, he will probably vomit a couple of pints of blood into your face. It can be really messy, but when it is done, that is it. This vampire will never wake up again, and if you killed an ancient vampire, he will turn to dust in front of your eyes.

Fire. Fire will also kill a vampire. Put some chains around the coffin and set fire to it. But don't forget that a vampire has superhuman strength. There is a chance he will break the chains and escape from the flames in the shape of a bat.

Daylight. Another possibility is to drag him into the daylight while he is still inside his coffin. He will die all by himself. This is not the easiest method, though, because those coffins weigh a ton. So never do this alone!

Decapitation. Cutting off a vampire's head is seen as an excellent way of killing him too, usually in combination with a wooden stake through the heart. Here too, you must remember that it can only be done during the day when he is in his coffin, because if you come at night, you will find that the bird (bat) has flown the coop. And... you need to get your hands on a sharp axe first.

Silver bullet. If you find all that chopping and piercing too gory, there is another method: shoot the vampire with a silver bullet blessed by a priest. But you need to make sure the vampire does not get into the moonlight afterwards, because that can bring him back to life. Suppose you shoot a vampire on your doorstep in the middle of the night, you must drag him into your house. You can always explain it to your family later.

Garlic. Vampires can't bear garlic. No one really knows why. People have believed for centuries that garlic has special powers. In the first century, the Roman writer Pliny wrote a book called *Natural History*, in which he claimed that garlic helps keep snakes and scorpions

away. These animals can't stand the smell of garlic.

Vampires hate it too. Hang some garlic in front of your window and no vampire will dare to enter. If you find a vampire's coffin and you put a string of garlic into it, the vampire can't get back into his coffin. They have to find another place to hide before it gets light. Garlic is a way of making sure a vampire feels hunted down.

You can't kill vampires with garlic. You can only frighten them with it and protect yourself. But you have to be careful, as the following true story will show you.

In Stoke-on-Trent in 1973 a man died after choking on a clove of garlic in his sleep. The man was Polish and had moved to England. He believed that vampires were real. On his window sill he kept a pot of garlic and he had sprinkled salt around his bed. (Some people also think salt is a good protection against vampires.) The man had fallen asleep with a clove of garlic in his mouth and had choked on it. He had died of his own superstition.

In the *News of the World* from 20th December 1992 there was an article that won't have escaped the notice of a good vampirologist:

GARLIC MORE AND MORE POPULAR IN UK

Garlic smells bad. But for the Oldershaw Group, who sell their garlic to Sainsbury's, this doesn't matter. The firm is making a killing because of the increased sales of garlic in the UK. At least, that is what they say in *Sainsbury's Magazine*.

> Most Brits are not overly keen on garlic, because of the strong smell. And yet sales have gone up considerably in the last few years. The average consumption in kilos per household has gone up from 3.8 in 1984 to 5.9 in 1990.

The Oldershaw Group have seen their sales triple in the last two years. According to the magazine, it is the "supposed medicinal properties of garlic" that have caused this rise in popularity.

"Supposed medicinal properties"? A vampirologist knows better than that... Vampires will have been gnashing their teeth in anger when they read this article. The more garlic people eat, the longer it takes them to find a suitable victim.

Crucifixes. They say crucifixes scare off vampires, but a vampire hunter can't rely on this any more. The crucifix is a religious symbol and not all vampires believe in its power. For some vampires, when a crucifix touches their skin, it burns them and leaves a scorch mark. Others just laugh at it.

What happens if you kill a vampire?

Some vampires, the very old ones, turn to dust if you kill them. Their skin shrivels up like an autumn leaf and flakes off their bones until only their skeleton is left. The bones then crumble until they are nothing but a little heap of dust. When someone has not been a vampire for so long, they retain their shape when they die. Their fangs disappear and they look like they did before they became a vampire. Except that now they are dead for good.

Where did it all start?

The vampire we know from most stories, and which we have been describing, originally came from Eastern Europe. In Romania in the sixteenth century they began telling stories about bloodthirsty creatures who came out of their graves at night looking for blood. They were described as big, rough characters with red faces who attacked people. They called them "vampire" or "nos-feratu" ("undead"). They thought they were responsible for all sorts of horrible diseases people were dying of back then. In the countryside, people would nail wreaths of garlic above their windows to keep out the vampires.

In Eastern Europe people still believe in vampires, especially in the Balkans. At some funerals they make sure a dead person can't return as a vampire by burying them with garlic in their mouth or nailing the corpse to the bottom of the coffin.

The very first bloodsuckers

A very long time ago people already believed in blood-sucking monsters, except that they weren't called vampires. More than two thousand years ago the Greeks told stories about the Lamia, the female ancestor of the "modern" vampire. She looked like a winged snake with the breasts and head of a woman. First she would drink a child's blood and then eat it. Even before that, people in Assyria (what is now northern Iraq) believed in a vampire-like ghost called Ekimmu who would rip its victims to shreds. Compared to this lot, "modern" vampires are real softies.

Dracula, the most famous vampire of all

If we imagine a vampire as a pale-faced aristocrat wearing a black cape and living in an ancient, ruined castle, this is because of Count Dracula, the most famous of all vampires. He overshadows all other vampires, although strictly speaking he doesn't cast a shadow, of course. Dracula made vampires really famous and feared the world over.

Dracula was thought up by the Irish writer Bram Stoker. He used Romanian stories about vampires that prowled graveyards as inspiration for his book *Dracula*. But he turned the vampire into a nobleman who lived in an ancient castle. *Dracula* was published in 1897 and has been reprinted many times. You can still buy it in bookshops now.

The story is about Count Dracula who lives in Transylvania in Romania. Transylvania means "the land beyond the forest". It is a wild region with lots of mountains and forests. Dracula is a four-hundred-year-old vampire who one day decides to leave his castle. He moves to England to continue his vampire activities. You can read more about Dracula in Chapters 8 and 9.

The name Dracula is world-famous. Almost everyone has heard of him. He is as famous as Santa Claus, except that he doesn't bring presents! He is after your blood!

Vampires are all the rage

More than two hundred films have been made about Dracula, and more are still being made (see Chapter 8). The story has been adapted for the stage and made into radio plays and even ballets. Comic strips about Dracula appear regularly, and there are also pieces of music that have been composed about him. There is a "bloody" good song called 'Love Song for a Vampire' by Annie Lennox. It is from the film *Bram Stoker's Dracula* (1992). Bram Stoker's book started a

craze that is still ongoing. In England there is a Dracula Society whose members celebrate the birthday of Bram Stoker, Dracula's creator, every year on 8th November.

In New York there is the Count Dracula Fan Club, which publishes its own magazine. Inspired by the original Dracula, there are also films about a black vampire called Blacula. Even *Sesame Street* has its own toddler version of Dracula: Count von Count – also just known as Count Count – who teaches children simple maths.

The vampire industry

Thanks to Dracula we now have vampire tourism. Travel agents organize horror trips to Romania, which is seen as *the* country for vampires since *Dracula* was first published. There, the horror fan can spend the night in the Dracula Hotel, built on the Borgo Pass, where part of the Dracula story is set. In souvenir shops you can buy Dracula dolls, Dracula fangs, bats and masks. There are Dracula toy cars, stickers, jigsaw puzzles, T-shirts and video games, as well as Dracula sweets and cornflakes. They even have Dracula toothpaste. In short, this one count is responsible for a whole vampire industry.

Vlad, the real Dracula

The man Bram Stoker used as a model for Dracula was a very cruel tyrant from the fifteenth century who lived in Wallachia, a province of Transylvania, in Romania. They called him Vlad Dracula. He was born in 1431 and died in 1476. Between 1448 and 1476 he was Prince of Wallachia. He was kicked out a few times, but each time he got back into power. Dracula means "the son of the dragon" or "the son of the devil". He was a member of the Order of the Dragon, whose symbol was a dragon, the Dracul.

Vlad was a bloodthirsty tyrant who brutally killed not only his enemies, but also his fellow countrymen – beggars, peasants and anyone he didn't like. No vampire could ever kill as many people as this human monster did.

The main character in Bram Stoker's book has the same name, and a large part of the book is set in

Transylvania. But the events in the book itself were made up by the author.

Popular hero

These days, many Romanians see Vlad Dracula as a kind of national hero, because he won many battles for their country and defeated the Turks. They want to improve his image. In 1976 they brought out a stamp with a picture of Vlad Dracula. The former dictator Ceausescu even had plans to restore Vlad Dracula's castle and live there himself. But he was executed by his army in 1989. Just in time, probably, because Romanians used to call Ceausescu "the Vampire".

Could it be that?...

The real Dracula has been dead for five centuries, but he has not been forgotten. In America they sell lockets with Vlad Dracula's portrait. The locket also contains a little bit of earth from the town of Sighişoara in Transylvania, where Vlad Dracula was born. That is strangely similar to the idea that vampires always keep a bit of the earth from where they were born in their coffin.

For the real horror fan it gets even more bizarre: in 1931 they opened the tomb where Vlad Dracula was supposed to lie. They found the skeletons of two different people. But neither of them was Vlad. His corpse

has disappeared, and no one has ever found it. Could it be that Vlad Dracula was a real vampire after all?...

Vampire bat

There is one vampire that really exists. It is about ten centimetres long and lives in South America. Its name is *Desmodus rotundus*, the common vampire bat. This little animal feeds on the blood of larger animals, like cows and horses. With its small, sharp teeth it bites its victims, after which it licks up their blood with its tongue. It only needs a tiny amount of blood, and the cow or horse doesn't notice a thing. The real danger of this vampire is that it can spread diseases such as rabies.

This bat has very little to do with vampires you find in books. It was only nicknamed vampire because it drinks the blood of living animals.

New vampire stars

You may wonder why people have been fascinated by vampires for so long. They are living corpses whose breath stinks of blood and who have some pretty disgusting habits. They try to bite you and drink your blood. Not the kind of people you would invite to your birthday party. And yet, vampires are about as popular as they were one hundred and twenty years ago. In recent times, one vampire has become almost as popular as Dracula, at least in America. His name is Lestat, who is a famous rock star as well as a vampire. His adventures are told in books written for adults by the American writer Anne Rice, collectively known as *The Vampire Chronicles*. The first book in the series is called *Interview with the Vampire* (1976), later made into a famous film starring Tom Cruise and Brad Pitt (1994). In it, the vampire Lestat tells his life story to a journalist. After that, the series continues with eleven more novels, the last of which – *Prince Lestat and the Realms of Atlantis* – is to be released later this year (2016). These are hefty tomes in which the vampire Lestat travels back in time and eventually returns to Ancient Egypt to find out more about his origins. They are not easy to read, but the horror fans who want to tackle them will really have something meaty to sink their teeth into.

More recently, new vampires and vampire hunters have been vying with Dracula and Lestat for stardom status. They have appeared in popular films and TV series such as *Buffy the Vampire Slayer* (1992, 1997–2003), *Let the Right One In* (2008), *The Twilight Saga* (2008–12), *True Blood* (2008–14), *Thirst* (2009), *The Vampire Diaries* (started in 2009) and many more. Most of them loosely model themselves on vampire books that were around before.

Lonely and frightening

Maybe we are fascinated by vampires because they have something we don't have: they live for ever. But I don't think anyone would allow themselves to be bitten by a vampire just so they can become a vampire too. The idea of having to live from century to century, being forced to drink a few litres of blood every day to keep your strength up, is not really very attractive. In addition, as a vampire you have to stay hidden, because there are people hunting you. Sometimes vampires must get tired of their eternal, dark existence.

In a way, vampires are lonely figures who restlessly wander through the ages. Lonely and frightening, maybe that is why they are so interesting. But would you want to trade places with one?

3
Werewolves

Fleete could not speak, he could only snarl, and his snarls were those of a wolf, not of a man. The human spirit must have been giving way all day and have died out with the twilight. We were dealing with a beast that had once been Fleete.

'The Mark of the Beast', by Rudyard Kipling

The night is clear and a full moon is shining high up in the sky. Suddenly the silence is shattered by a blood-curdling howl. A noise no human could possibly make. Don't be pig-headed, don't be brave, don't think: "Hey, let's go and see what is going on there." Go home, lock your doors and windows and crawl into your bed. If you don't, chances are that someone will find you the next morning in a park, with your body parts scattered all over the place like bloody pieces of a jigsaw puzzle. A werewolf will have struck.

The werewolf is an important member of the horror family. His contribution to the art of horror goes back a long time. Centuries ago people got the shivers when the moon was full and they heard a wolf howling in the distance. They knew: tonight we had better stay indoors because there is a werewolf on the loose. There are stories about werewolves all over the world, especially in countries where wolves once lived. People have always been afraid of wolves, and stories about werewolves were probably born out of fear. Often the werewolf was used as a bogeyman to scare children who wouldn't listen: "Don't go out tonight because a werewolf will come and get you."

What is a werewolf?

Werewolves are not men that *were* wolves at some point, or the other way round, but people who, once a month, when the moon is full, change into a wolf, usually without being able to do anything about it. The rest of the time, they are ordinary people who spend their days working in a bank, say in Leeds, or in London, or perhaps Llandudno. But at night, when the moon is full, these seemingly respectable gentlemen are transformed into bloodthirsty monsters looking for humans or animals to kill. No one is safe when they are on the prowl. Both men and women can be werewolves, although in most stories female werewolves are very rare.

What does a werewolf look like?

Werewolf means wolf-man. The word "were" comes from the Old English "wer", which means "man" or "male person". A werewolf is bigger and looks fiercer than a real wolf. According to some ancient stories, only the eyes stay human. Those eyes look yellow in the moonlight.

Transformation

The most important thing about a werewolf is his transformation: when a man changes into a werewolf. It is worth having a closer look.

The night is clear and a beautiful full moon is shining. This is the time of their transformation.

There, in an isolated bit of a park, stands our respectable bank clerk. The last few nights, he has been restless, because the moon was almost full. He knows that the wolf in him wants to come out. He has been feeling itchy and has been scratching himself for days. The night has finally arrived. When the moon rose earlier that evening, he couldn't contain himself any longer. It was as if the moon were calling him. Like a madman he ran into the park, where he wouldn't be seen. And there he stands, waiting for what is about to take place next. He tilts his head to face the moon. Then it happens. His clothes rip open. From the torn sleeves two hairy arms emerge. His hands change into claws. His feet burst out of their shoes and become wolf's paws with long claws. From his throat comes a sound that is no longer human, first a savage snarl and then a beastly howl. The transformation is extremely painful. His nose gets longer and changes into a wolf's muzzle. His ears become pointy and hairy. Whatever is left of his clothes is too tight now, and he rips everything off in a fury. Instead of a bank clerk, a wolf is standing there on all fours. Once again he tilts his head towards the moon and a blood-curdling howl sounds through the night like a cry of joy and liberation. The werewolf has broken out! He has been freed from his human form. That night he goes on a murderous rampage. Anyone who meets the werewolf is doomed. The werewolf is consumed by a blind rage. He no longer thinks like a human being. He hates people and all he wants to do is tear them to pieces.

When the moon disappears, he returns to his human form. The next morning the werewolf is unaware of the godawful things he has done. Surprised, he asks himself what on earth happened to his clothes as he wakes up shivering and naked at the entrance of the bank where he works.

This is the most famous and most common transformation you will find in modern werewolf stories and films, like the scary and funny film *An American Werewolf In London* (1981).

Full moon. In most stories, someone can only change into a werewolf once a month: when the moon is full. Maybe this belief is linked to the idea of lunacy (from the Latin word for moon, "luna"). People used to believe that under the influence of the moon you could have  nervous breakdowns, sleepwalk and even have attacks of madness.

Bloodlust. The scary thing about werewolves is their rage. It is a furious rage mainly directed at human beings. Someone may be a very kind person, but once he turns into a werewolf he becomes a murderous beast. Generally speaking, werewolves are unhappy with their lot, which they can do nothing about.

A helper of vampires

Werewolves used to be seen as helpers of vampires. People thought there was a connection between them. But there are important differences between these two brothers of the horror family. Vampires are undead. They are living corpses. But a werewolf is a normal human being most of the time.

Vampires are able to change into wolves. And in Greece and France people used to think werewolves became vampires after their death.

How do you recognize a werewolf?

Because a werewolf is a normal person during the day, it is very difficult to spot one. Except if you know what to look for. In the sixteenth century, the belief in werewolves was widespread, and people saw them everywhere. What happened was that stories about an "alternative reality" became mixed up with real life.

Anyone who looks "different". In countries like Portugal, France and Greece, they thought you could recognize a werewolf by the colour and shape of someone's eyes. People with bright eyes might be werewolves, or else with very dark eyes. Red hair was suspect, as was flaxen hair, or a monobrow. If your index and middle finger were the same length, you would be looked at with suspicion. Or if your middle finger was extra long. Or if you had long, curved nails, or teeth that stuck out, or a narrow face, sunken eyes, a pale complexion. Or if your ears were a little pointy at the top, or a bit lower on your head compared with other people.

And of course, if you were very hairy, people were bound to suspect you, especially if you had hair on your hands and feet. In the sixteenth century, anyone who looked different in one way or another was treated as a possible werewolf. Especially people with a physical deformity such as a hunchback or someone with a cleft lip.

If you stick to these rules and look carefully around you, you will be surprised to see that our streets are teeming with potential werewolves. These prejudices were born out of fear – fear for anything that is different. It is the same stupid fear that makes people hate foreigners and become racist. Sometimes it seems as if we were back in the sixteenth century.

In that period, many people suspected of being werewolves were burnt at the stake, especially in France. In the same period, thousands of people were burnt as witches (see Chapter 6).

The milkman test. In the "alternative reality" of the art of horror, there is only one good way to catch out werewolves when they have their human form. If you hurt a werewolf when he is a wolf, for example by scratching his eye, and the next day the milkman appears with a patch over his eye, then he is almost certainly a werewolf. So remember: the milkman test.

How do you become a werewolf?

A werewolf's bite. One bite by a werewolf is enough to change someone into one too. This is the vampire method. But there is a difference. The vampire bites his victims multiple times and drinks his or her blood until they die. Only then does the victim become a real vampire. The werewolf is not a bloodsucker. Someone who is bitten by a werewolf only becomes one if they happen to survive the attack.

Pact with the devil. In some old stories people became werewolves after they made a deal with the Devil. They were often witches who promised to worship and obey the Devil. In exchange, they got the power to transform themselves into wolves. They became werewolves of their own free will.

According to some, witches and sorcerers were also able to change other people into werewolves through magic.

A wolf skin. There were also people who chose to become werewolves by dressing themselves in the skin of a wolf. They had been given the wolf skin by the Devil in exchange for their soul.  They enjoyed running around like fierce wolves, tearing other people to pieces. They would hide their wolf skin in a hollow tree and get it out when the moon was full. When they put on the wolf skin, they became werewolves.

Sometimes the Devil or other werewolves would force people to put on a wolf skin and do evil things as a werewolf. The Devil must have kept an unlimited supply of wolf skins in his wardrobe.

Magic ointment. In France, Germany and Scandinavia people used to believe you could change into a werewolf by rubbing magic ointment onto your skin. This ointment, or salve, was made from the fat of a dead cat, the blood of a bat, aniseed and opium. From time to time, they would also mix in the blood of a child – *mwahahaha*.

A belt of human skin. Other things that worked well were a belt made from human skin, preferably a murderer's, or from wolf hair. Or else a wolf-skin shirt. When you put on the belt or shirt and said the secret magic words, you would change into a werewolf. This transformation was usually someone's own choice too.

Eating and drinking. Sometimes it was enough to drink water from the footprints of a wolf or eat a wolf's brain, either because you wanted to, or because you were forced.

A cursed family. When a werewolf had children, the chances were that his children would later become werewolves too. In that case the family was cursed, and this curse was passed on from father to son. The curse would be lifted when the werewolf was killed.

Lycanthropy. Sometimes werewolves are called lycanthropes, but in reality a lycanthrope (Greek for "wolf-man") is just a person who *thinks* he is a wolf. He walks around on all fours and growls and howls like a wolf.

How do you kill or free a werewolf?

Silver bullet. You can kill a werewolf with a silver bullet. If you want, you can have the bullet blessed by a priest first. This is the most common way, and always successful. If you aim right, of course. As soon as he is dead, the werewolf changes back into a human being, although unfortunately a dead one.

According to some stories, werewolves are afraid of anything made of silver. So, if you are walking about at night, make sure you have a silver coin or spoon in your pocket. You never know, it could come in handy.

In most modern werewolf books and films, the silver bullet is seen as the only means of killing a werewolf. In *Silver Bullet*, an American film from 1985 based on a short story by Stephen King (the world-famous American writer of horror stories whose books have sold more than 350 million copies worldwide), a disabled boy kills a werewolf with a silver bullet.

In older stories, there are a few other ways of making sure a werewolf is no longer dangerous without actually killing him.

Burn their wolf skin. Werewolves who use a wolf skin don't have to be killed. It is enough to set fire to their wolf skin. Of course, you will have to find the hollow tree where they hide it first.

While the skin is burning, the owner will be in agony and suffer awful pains, even if he is miles away. But when the skin has turned to ashes, he will be free and will never be a werewolf again. He will be for ever grateful, except if he became a werewolf of his own free will. In that case it is just tough luck.

Stuff its mouth with a handkerchief. If you meet a werewolf and you don't happen to have a silver bullet or a silver spoon on you, you can always stuff your hanky or shirt into its mouth. While it is busy picking the cloth from between its fangs, you can make your escape. If a werewolf eats the clothes of an innocent child, he will be free from the spell.

Call his human name. There are stories that say that it is enough to call out someone's human name when he is a werewolf. It works like a magic spell, and the werewolf changes back immediately. Of course you would need to know who the werewolf is – for instance by using the "milkman test".

Three drops of blood. Sometimes, all you need to do is to draw three drops of blood while the werewolf is human. In this case too, you need to use the "milkman test" to figure out who he is.

Kind words. In Denmark they believed you could cure a werewolf by speaking kind and understanding words to it, like you do when you are friendly to a dog. Since most werewolves would literally be at your throat before you can open your mouth to say anything, it is no doubt safest to address the werewolf from a tall tree.

What is the origin of the belief in werewolves?

People in animal skins. The first stories about werewolves come from Greece. The Ancient Greeks used to tell many stories about Arcadia, a region in Greece which had many wolves, and that is where the oldest werewolf story is from. In other countries they also had stories about people who could change into animals. But they didn't become werewolves but other "were-animals".

In India they believed in "weretigers". In Russia they were convinced there were "werebears" as well as werewolves, and in Africa they told stories about "werecrocodiles" and "werepanthers". At the beginning of the twentieth century, there was a secret society in Africa called the Leopard Society, whose members dressed in leopard skins and believed they had the power and the mind of a leopard.

People have been wearing animal skins for a very long time, to protect themselves against the cold, but also to frighten their enemies by behaving like a wolf, a leopard or some such animal. A famous example of this are the Berserkers from Old Norse stories. They were warriors who dressed in bear skins and would roam the country, robbing and stealing what they could. They would roar like bears and often froth at the mouth, making their victims think they were being attacked by crazy bears. That is why we say someone is going berserk if they get out of control with anger or excitement and start acting like they are crazy. It is likely that the belief in werewolves, in addition to our fear of wolves, has something to do with these fancy-dress parties.

The werewolf conquers the world. European merchants took their werewolf stories with them as they travelled all over the world. In other countries they started repeating these stories, or they changed them a little to suit their own culture.

And so, little by little, the myth of the werewolf has conquered the entire world.

The oldest werewolf story. The belief in werewolves is much older even than the belief in vampires. The oldest werewolf story can be found in the Ancient

Greek myths, stories about gods and heroes that are thousands of years old.

The original werewolf story is about king Lycaon, a cruel ruler who was nasty to his people and ate so much that he looked like a stuffed pig. Zeus, the king of the Greek gods, couldn't stand it any longer. He disguised himself as a human and came down to earth to punish Lycaon. Once he had come to earth, he told Lycaon who he was. But the evil king didn't believe him and laughed in the god's face, because he looked like an ordinary person. "If you are a god, then I am the king of the wolves," he said. To test if Zeus was really a god, Lycaon prepared a meal for him. He cooked up a child he had murdered himself. When Zeus discovered this, he was furious and changed Lycaon into a wolf to punish him. And that is how Lycaon became the ancestor of all werewolves.

What is a typical werewolf story?

Most werewolf stories have a simple plot. A series of mysterious murders have taken place. People and animals are found with their bodies torn to pieces. The police want to find out who is behind this. Inspector van Loon is at his wits' end as to who might have done these horrendous things. With his assistant Didden he starts an investigation, but it doesn't lead anywhere.

A month later there is another series of similar murders. The village lives in fear. Children are no longer allowed to go out by themselves. They have to be home before dark. After the third series of murders, Inspector van Loon makes a discovery. The murders always happen at full moon. The next time the moon is full, Van Loon lies in wait in his car armed with a gun. As it happens, his assistant Didden can't come with him that evening because his mother had to be rushed off to the hospital unexpectedly. Inspector van Loon is all alone, but he is not one to give up very easily. And sure enough, around midnight he sees a wolf prowling the empty streets. Van Loon doesn't hesitate. He takes aim and shoots. Unfortunately he only hits its right front paw and the animal escapes, howling with pain.

The next morning Van Loon tells Didden what happened. As for Didden, he showed up to work that morning with his right hand bandaged...

The plot of this story shows that the "milkman test" always works.

Anyone who has read this example and thinks: "I can do better than that and come up with a much more original werewolf story" – well, what are you waiting for? Write it down. Stories about werewolves could use some new blood!

Werewolf legends

In books with old myths and legends you will read werewolf stories that are very different from modern books and films. In them, werewolves don't just attack humans, but are up to all sorts of weird tricks.

In one story, a werewolf sits down on the doorstep of a house waiting for everyone to fall asleep. When they do, he breaks into the house to steal their food. This werewolf is nothing but a plain old burglar.

In other stories, werewolves jump on people's backs and ride along for a couple of miles or so. After that, they disappear. They usually pick the same person more than once, but only want to be carried on their back. They don't do them any harm. No one knows why they behave this way.

One old story tells the tale of a werewolf who used to show himself to people in the middle of the night and do strange tricks. He would dance, walk on his front paws, do cartwheels, as if he were in a circus. When the performance was over, he skedaddled.

Sometimes a werewolf would come to the rescue

when people were being attacked by highwaymen. Maybe he hoped his good deed would lift the curse.

There were even werewolves with a bizarre sense of humour. According to one short story, there was a werewolf who used to hide in a river, waiting for people to come by in the evening. As soon as they approached, he would come out of the water, shake his fur and drench the people. After that, he would walk away, laughing his head off.

Young werewolves. A simple explanation for the existence of stories about werewolves is that they show the evil that is inside of us all. Werewolves do naughty things we civilized people can't do. Secretly everyone would like to be a werewolf every once in a while and do wild things.

There is a great picture book for children by Maurice Sendak that shows this very clearly: *Where the Wild Things Are* (1963). In this classic story, Max puts on his wolf costume when he is being naughty. In reality, what he is doing is the same as what those old werewolves did when they took their wolf skin out of their hollow trees and changed into werewolves to do terrible things. But Max is not the only young werewolf to appear in children's books. Take, for example, the mysterious wolf-boy in 'Gabriel-Ernest' (1910), a short story by the British writer Saki.

Staying power

All things considered, you have to admit that the werewolf has staying power. Even though people have been trying to destroy him for centuries, he keeps on cropping up in books and films. Like the vampire, he is indestructible. We all have a little bit of werewolf inside of us. So next time the moon is full, be on your guard…

4

Ghosts

Opening my eyes, which I had shut while recovering my firmness, I now met in the glass, looking straight at me, the eyes of a young man of four- or five-and-twenty. Terrified by this new ghost, I closed my eyes, and made a strong effort to recover myself. Opening them again, I saw, shaving his cheek in the glass, my father, who has long been dead.

From 'The Ghost in Master B.'s Room', by Charles Dickens

The art of horror probably started with ghost stories. The oldest horror stories are about ghosts and spirits who come from the realm of the dead and show themselves to the living. A spirit is immaterial, which means it is not made of flesh and blood. It can walk straight through walls, but it can't touch you. Nothing to be afraid of, you would say, but meeting the spirit of an uncle who has been dead for ten years will give most people goose bumps or even a heart attack. If someone has had a real fright, you say they look like they have seen a ghost.

Another word for spirit is ghost or phantom. But not all spirits are ghosts or phantoms. A ghost or phantom is always the spirit of someone who died, while a spirit can also be something else, for example an invisible power like a poltergeist. Stories about spirits are called ghost stories. I know this is a little bit confusing, but no one has come up with the term "spirit story" in English. Many ghost stories belong to an "alternative reality", but for centuries there have been tales about people who have really seen or heard ghosts...

Phantoms or ghosts

Phantoms or ghosts are the spirits of dead people who still wander around on earth. They look exactly like the person who died, except you can't grab them. They are deathly pale and often even transparent. Sometimes they are people who died a tragic death and were murdered, for example, or who had an accident. These ghosts keep returning to the place where they died. Maybe because they can't forget what happened and are still unhappy about it. There are also ghosts who were terrible people when they were alive: murderers, robber barons and other wicked characters. When people like this die, they can't find peace and keep coming back to the crime scene, but as ghosts. When they appear, they usually bring with them an ice-cold current of air.

What do ghosts look like?

You can see through them. Ghosts or phantoms still look the way they did when they were alive. So they look like ordinary people and wear all the same things. They wear the clothes, shoes and hats from the period they lived in, except that it is all a bit transparent, because they are spirits now.

Knights and damsels. Old castles are the favourite haunts for knights in armour. You will also find lots of damsels in swishing dresses. In old abbeys and monasteries you are more likely to find monks with large hoods covering their heads.

Headless ghosts. It is even scarier when you meet the spirit of someone who died a terrible death. Ghosts of people who were beheaded walk around with a bleeding stump where their head used to be and carry their heads

under their arms. Ghosts of people who were hanged usually appear with a noose around their neck and hold their head at an angle. There are also ghosts who look like charred corpses, or who have cleft skulls or swords sticking out of their bodies. If you meet one of them, you will know how they died.

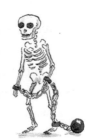

In chains. Ghosts of criminals must often pay for the terrible things they have done, and wander from one place to the next, dragging their heavy chains with them, often moaning and groaning pitifully.

Half-ghosts and invisible spirits. What happens every now and again is that only one half of a ghost appears, or only one part is visible, like a floating upper body, a head or a dragging foot. Why they do this is a mystery. Some spirits never show themselves. They only make noises: footsteps, voices, whispers. Perhaps they are just shy.

Bones. Some spirits only have bones. They have lost their human shape and appear as skeletons. You can easily recognize them by the rattling noise their bones make.

A sheet with holes in. Everyone knows about phantoms that look like a sheet with two holes for eyes. This type of phantom appears mostly in fairy tales, stories for young children and as a shelf label in bookshops and libraries to tell readers they have picked up a ghost story. Just like the fangs are the

vampire's symbol, the sheet with holes in it is the phantom's symbol. In reality it is very unlikely that a spirit will show itself as a sheet, unless it is the spirit of someone who died smothered by a sheet after the laundry basket fell on top of them.

Burning ghosts

In some old stories there are burning ghosts that are made up of flames. These ghosts burn as a form of punishment, for example because they treated people badly while they were alive. They are nasty and come at you with terrifying speed if you are stupid enough to call them. If you manage to slam the door in their face, you will find a charred imprint of a hand on your door the next day. If you ask a burning ghost to light a fire, you set him free. There is one disadvantage, though: you will take over the curse and instantaneously change into a burning ghost yourself.

Ghouls

Ghouls are evil spirits from Arabian folklore that supposedly roam around cemeteries and feed on human flesh. They appear in works such as the *One Thousand and One Nights* and C.S. Lewis's *The Lion, the Witch and the Wardrobe* (1950). In more recent times, the word "ghoul" has come to describe any undead monster that creates havoc and has a streak for real nastiness.

Animal ghosts

There are many kinds of animal ghosts too: ghost cats, ghost dogs, ghost hares, ghost horses and so on. Sometimes animal ghosts are the pets of people who died and returned as ghosts. In the TV film *Ghost Cat* (2003), the ghost of a cat is haunting the house in which it died on the same day as its owner.

In England, they used to have black ghost dogs as big as calves. They had names like Black Shuck, Yeth and Gytrash and sowed fear in anyone travelling late at night with their howling. Very strange animal ghosts – could they be real? – also appear in *The Hound of the Baskervilles* (1902) by Arthur Conan Doyle and in *The Nature of the Beast* (1985) by Janni Howker.

Ghost objects and vehicles

There are also stories about ghostly objects. These are items or vehicles that somehow have a link to something that happened in the past: the possessions of a murderer or someone who was murdered, vehicles people were killed in, bells of churches that have been destroyed and so forth.

Chairs may appear out of nowhere at specific moments. There are ghost bells that ring mysteriously, ghost trains, ghost cars and ghost coaches drawn by black horses with flaming eyes.

Ghost ships

Things can get spooky at sea too. Literally. Sailors tell stories of ghost ships that appear out of the depths of the ocean on stormy nights. In the film *The Fog* (1980), a ship that was wrecked one hundred years before appears

near a small village on the coast. The ghosts on board the ship have come to take revenge for something that happened a century ago.

A famous ghost ship is the *Flying Dutchman*. They used to say that you would die or go blind if you ever looked at the ship when it appeared. Another one is the ghost ship of Northumberland Strait, which has been sighted for over two hundred years as it sails ablaze off the coast of Nova Scotia in Canada, presumably heading towards the coolness of the Arctic waters.

Images from the past

In 1908 Sir Oliver Lodge wrote in his book *Man and the Universe* that ghosts are like a recording from the past. Something that happened in the past is repeated all the time, like when you are showing a film. If you see a ghost, in a way you are looking at the past. This theory is called "retroscopia" (which means "looking back").

In *Harry Potter and the Deathly Hallows* (2007), the last of the Harry Potter series of novels, Snape gives Harry his last memories to be viewed on a "pensieve" device. This will enable Harry to discover a terrible secret and a way to overcome his arch-enemy Voldemort.

Why do ghosts show themselves?

Unsolved mysteries. Ghosts don't show themselves without a reason. In some cases they are trying to tell the living something, often about an unsolved mystery. In a sixteenth-century castle in Scotland, people regularly saw the ghost of a woman with a baby on her arm. This woman and her baby were murdered by the lord of the castle a long time ago. When one day, during a restoration, they removed an iron plate at the back of a fireplace, they found the skeletons of a young woman and a baby.

When a discovery like that is made, ghosts usually stop appearing. At least if their bodies are given a proper burial in a cemetery. At last they have found peace.

They don't know that they are dead. There are ghosts who appear because they don't know they are dead. They just haven't noticed or figured it out. That is why they continue to visit the same places they used to go to. Until they realize that they are dead, like the ghost in the following story.

Nathaniel Hawthorne, a nineteenth-century American writer, used to have lunch every day in the same restaurant. On the table next to him, a certain Doctor Harris would always be reading the newspaper. They didn't know each other and never talked. One day, the writer went on holiday, and when he returned to the restaurant, sure enough, Doctor Harris was there, as always, reading his newspaper. Later that day, Hawthorne heard that Doctor Harris had been dead for days – dead and buried. After that, Doctor Harris appeared a few more times and then it stopped. He had probably cottoned on to the fact that he was dead.

Punishment. The spirits of criminals are often forced to wander around for ever without finding peace. This is a punishment for their crimes. It sometimes happens that a ghost like that will try to make up for his sins, for example by indicating where a stolen object is hidden or where a missing corpse can be found. If he is successful, he can be pardoned after a few centuries or so, and he will be at peace. He won't have to wander around as a ghost any more.

Revenge. Another reason ghosts return is to take revenge on someone who did something to them. Or just because they are plain evil. An example of this is the Green Lady, a vengeful female spirit whose favourite haunts are some fairly remote castles in Scotland.

Ghostly tasks. Some ghosts return because they have to finish something or carry out a task before they can find peace.

Warning. Sometimes ghosts appear to warn someone that something terrible is going to happen. A disaster, for example, or a fatal accident.

Which places are haunted?

Ghosts usually appear in houses where they used to live as people, or where they were murdered. Places where ghosts appear are said to be "haunted". There are many haunted castles. There are stories about haunted houses and castles all over the world, but England is without a doubt the country with the most ghosts.

The country is full of castles, manors and other buildings that are haunted. An ordinary Englishman is not in the least bit surprised to find that there are strange noises coming from the attic of his terraced house. He will calmly finish his tea and when a transparent lady comes down the stairs he will offer her a drink ever so courteously. They say that in most English homes, there are as many ghosts as there are mice. The English simply *adore* ghosts. They grow up listening to ghost stories and keep the tradition going.

For those who like ghost stories, there are special guidebooks with maps on which you can find the most famous haunted houses.

The Tower of London. The most famous and notorious haunted castle is the Tower of London, where the Crown Jewels are kept. It is a building with a bloody past. Many noblemen and women were beheaded there, or murdered in some other fashion – and, they say, they all haunt the Tower.

Anne Boleyn, Henry VIII's second wife, is often seen, sometimes with, sometimes without her head.

In 1541 Margaret Pole, the Countess of Salisbury, was sentenced to be killed with an axe by an executioner. After the first clumsy blow, which hit her shoulder, the countess ran away from the execution block, and the executioner only managed to cut off her head after a wild chase. Some nights you can see her ghost running across the lawn, with the executioner on her heels, swinging his axe.

The so-called Bloody Tower is haunted by the Princes in the Tower, the sons of King Edward IV, who were murdered there in 1483.

And E.L. Swift, the former keeper of the Crown Jewels, claims he saw a number of floating objects in the Martin Tower once: a glass tube filled with a strange liquid hovering around the room.

As famous as the Tower itself are the ravens that are kept there. I need to give you a warning at this point. Stay well clear of the ravens, because if you kill one, by mistake or on purpose, you will come to a sticky end!

In Michael Morpurgo's *My Friend Walter* (1988) a girl befriends a sixteenth-century ghost in the Tower and even takes him home.

Ghost Bus Tours. There are innumerable ghosts in the whole of Great Britain, not just in England, from singing Welsh phantom minstrels to bagpipe-playing Scottish ghosts.

In London you can take the Jack the Ripper, Haunted London and Sherlock Holmes Tour. An open-top double-decker bus will take you to places where people were murdered by the Ripper or that are still haunted. With a bit of luck, you may have your own personal ghost travelling with you on the bus.

Frankenstein Castle. In Darmstadt, in Germany, you can visit Frankenstein Castle. The name Frankenstein became famous because of the monster in the film *Frankenstein* (1931), after Mary Shelley's novel of 1818.

When she was young, Mary visited Frankenstein Castle and later used that name in her book about the monster.

Every year, on the eve of All Saints' Day – the night between 31st October and 1st November – they throw a Hallowe'en party at Frankenstein Castle. The origin of the name Hallowe'en is All Hallows' Evening ("hallow" meaning "holy"). According to an ancient superstition, that night, all evil spirits and monsters are released from Hell and allowed to wander around and spook people. Thousands of horror fans from all over Europe are bussed into Darmstadt, dressed up as vampires, witches and, of course, Frankenstein's monster, to celebrate this huge monster party. They sell creepy postcards and books with new adventures of Frankenstein's monster, written by a local primary-school teacher.

A long time ago, according to some stories, strange things took place in this German castle. It used to be notorious because of two monsters that were supposed to live in it. The first was a gigantic bat, the pet of one of the lords of Frankenstein Castle. It would feed on the blood of people near the castle. They killed the bat, but it returned after its death as a kind of vampire ghost. It was still sometimes seen in the twentieth century.

The second monster was a dragon, which was killed in 1531 by Sir Georg von Frankenstein. More than three centuries later, in 1852, the dragon's ghost appeared on Hallowe'en near Sir Georg's tomb. The castle is also haunted by the ghosts of a number of lords who used to live there. But naturally, they pale into insignificance compared to the two monsters.

Ghost writers

Nowadays it is even possible to hear about ghost writers. There are many of these creatures at large in the publishing underworld – more than one would imagine. They are people who write books for other people. No one knows their names or even their faces, and they don't get any credit for what they write because someone else paid them to write the book and keep quiet about it, so they could pretend to be the author.

Phantom limbs

When someone's arm or leg is amputated, the brain does not always realize this, a bit like Nathaniel Hawthorne's doctor. You can still wriggle your toes even if you no longer have a foot. One man had his legs severed when he was driving his car and could never sleep in a normal bed again because he had the feeling his legs were sticking through the mattress. His phantom legs were still thinking they were sitting down in a car. Things can also get bad if you have a phantom itch, because how do you scratch an arm or leg that isn't even there?

In horror movies, some of these disembodied limbs – especially hands – wander around creating all sorts of mischief, as in the famous film *The Hand* (1981), directed by Oliver Stone and starring Michael Caine.

Ghostbusters

The most famous film about ghost hunters is almost certainly *Ghostbusters* (1984). In this film, three wacky scientists track down and capture ghosts for a living with the help of ultra-modern technology. But there are actual "ghostbusters" too, who take on ghosts and spirits with all sorts of equipment, from computers to microphones, cameras and even radars.

Many of these people work at universities and do very serious research into ghosts. They try to capture them on tape or on camera in order to have scientific proof that they exist. However, because spirits and ghosts are immaterial and usually transparent, it is virtually impossible to film or photograph them.

Real "ghostbusters" don't give up so easily, though. In England there has been a Ghost Club since 1862. Its members are not ghosts, but scientists. They regularly give lectures about spirits and sometimes organize trips to haunted houses to try and catch or meet one.

Invisible spirits

Spirits you can't see are even scarier than phantoms. The only way you know they are there is because you feel a sudden, ice-cold draught. You also know they are in the room if objects suddenly begin to move of their own accord.

Good and evil spirits. Especially in eastern countries like Japan and Indonesia, the belief in invisible spirits is still very strong. Every year, they organize events and practise rituals to drive away evil spirits that can spread disease or make the harvest fail. Good spirits are there to protect humans against the evil ones. To keep the good spirits happy, humans leave gifts in places where they are said to live, like forests and temples, but also in graveyards.

Poltergeists. A poltergeist is not a phantom, but an invisible spirit. The film director Steven Spielberg wrote and produced a film called *Poltergeist* in 1982. The word comes from the German "*poltern*" ("to crash" or "bang") and "*Geist*" ("spirit").

You can't see this spirit, but you know it is there because it behaves like a crazy carpenter or an angry child throwing a violent tantrum. Windows fly open, doors are slammed shut, objects fly through the air as if thrown by an invisible hand, lamps begin to swing on the ceiling and you can hear banging noises. Sometimes a poltergeist causes a terrible stench too.

Poltergeists are mysterious and have been around a long time. The oldest existing written description of it dates from 355 AD. In Bingen-am-Rhein something invisible started throwing stones at people and pushing them out of bed at night. In 1964 in Stow-on-the-Wold, so the story goes, a poltergeist wrote things on the wall and sang songs based on pop hits, but with its own lyrics.

Could poltergeists just be children? People have been looking for an explanation for poltergeists for a very long time. Researchers think they are somehow connected to children (who always get blamed for everything!). Without being aware of it, it is children who make these invisible forces appear.

If you have seen the film *Carrie* (1976), based on a book by Stephen King, you will know what I am talking about. In that film a girl can cause knives and forks to fly through the air without touching them.

Demons. Demons are evil spirits that want to hurt humans and force them to do wicked things. In the Middle Ages they were seen as hideous creatures with horns and claws, like little devils, but very often they are invisible. In the Middle Ages witches and sorcerers tried to make demons appear so they could use them to destroy their enemies.

Demonic possession

Demonic possession is when someone is in the power of a demon. As a result they are no longer in control of themselves.

Demonic possession was particularly common in the seventeenth century. When someone started to behave in a strange way, they believed that person was possessed by a demon. A demon, which is an invisible power, took possession of someone by sneaking into their body, as it were. Once inside, the demon was quite happy and wouldn't just allow itself to be chucked out.

A possessed person did things they would normally never do. They squirmed and rolled around on the ground, unable to control themselves. Sometimes they would speak in a strange voice or even in a foreign language, like Latin or Greek. The demon enjoyed making the possessed person curse and swear or use filthy words. In the film *The Exorcist* (1973), a possessed girl spins her head 360 degrees. No wonder that a little later she vomits out something that looks like mushy peas. It is not a very tasteful film, even for horror fans who like mushy peas.

Demonic possession also happens in voodoo, especially the kind of voodoo they have in Haiti (see Chapter 5).

Exorcists

As soon as someone was possessed, they would call an exorcist. These were people who knew how to get rid of a demon who had entered someone's body. They were usually priests or other clergymen, because they thought demons were a kind of devil and therefore enemies of the Church. The priests' task was to make sure that the devil left the body. They called this ritual "casting out demons". Another term for "casting out" is "exorcizing" – hence the word "exorcist".

Even now, there are cases of demonic possession and there are priests and clergymen who drive out demons. Sometimes one exorcist will do the trick, but there are times when more are needed. There was a case like that in England in 1974. As many as six exorcists were needed. Together they drove out the demon with prayers from the Bible, with the result that the evil spirit eventually left the body cursing and swearing. At least, that was what they thought. Because afterwards the man in question went home with his wife and killed her…

Rattles against evil spirits

A very ancient way of protecting young children against evil spirits is the rattle. Archaeologists have found rattles made of clay and wood dating from prehistoric times. With a rattle in its cot, a baby is protected, because evil spirits are scared off by the noise it makes. Rattles from the sixteenth and seventeenth centuries had bells and whistles attached to them to chase away evil spirits. Rattles made from special material were extra powerful: blood coral, wolf teeth, the tusks of a wild boar. They also often had a special form, like a dragon or a lion, to scare off evil spirits.

Who you gonna call?

You may have got the message by now. Spirits don't lift your spirits and ghosts are just plain ghastly. They may be great material for horror films or books, but you would rather not have one haunting your house. So if you are plagued by spirits, run to your nearest toy shop and buy a rattle. If they have sold out, Google your nearest ghostbusters and give them a ring. If you are visited by a skeleton with rattling bones, there is only one thing you can do: get yourself a dog.

5

The Walking Dead

I told them of the vault, and they pointed to the unbroken plaster wall and laughed. So I told them no more. They imply that I am a madman or a murderer - probably I am mad. But I might not be mad if those accursed tomb-legions had not been so silent.

From 'Herbert West - Reanimator', by H.P. Lovecraft

As well as the undead vampire, the horror family has another walking dead among its members, the zombie. He may not be quite as famous as Dracula, the werewolf or Frankenstein's monster, but he is part of the family all the same. The walking dead do something that is not supposed to be possible. While they should be lying in their coffins in their grave, they walk about as if they were alive. They are not ghosts or spirits, because you can see them clearly and even touch them (even though that is not a very clever thing to do). An obvious example of an "alternative reality", the horror fan will think, but just like witches, the walking dead actually exist in Haiti, the land of voodoo and zombies. Zombies can be frighteningly real.

What is a zombie?

A zombie is a dead person who has been taken from or has crawled out of their grave. It is a walking corpse with no soul, no will of its own, and yet it is made of flesh and blood.

You can recognize them by their empty staring eyes and their slow, shuffling way of walking, as if they were walking on slippery ice. It seems as if zombies don't hear, see or feel anything. They can't talk either. They just utter grunts that no one understands.

Zombies in films. In films, zombies often appear because a scientific experiment has gone wrong. A dangerous gas has escaped from a laboratory, for example, making the dead come out of their graves.

A famous zombie film is *Night of the Living Dead* (1968). The zombies in this film come out of their graves to eat the flesh of the living. Not really good for your appetite, then. Still, it was a very successful film (maybe especially with zombies), giving rise to five sequels and one prequel (see Chapter 8).

In a way, Frankenstein's monster can also be seen as a zombie. This pitiful character is made from the body parts of various different corpses, so in fact he is one of the walking dead too. Michael Jackson's video clip *Thriller* (1983) shows that zombies like to party from time to time. In the video clip, the dead leave their graves and not only do they shuffle about, they also dance like there is no tomorrow.

How does a film zombie behave? Your usual film zombie crawls from his grave. He normally looks like a rotting corpse with bits falling off all the time, although he doesn't seem to notice. Everyone who meets him runs away screaming. With some difficulty, he drags himself through the streets of densely populated modern cities looking for humans, because zombies eat human flesh, just like ogres in fairy tales. "Fee-fi-fo-fum, I smell the blood of an Englishman," says the ogre, but the zombie doesn't say a word. He can't talk, he can't hear you and he can't feel anything. Unstoppable, he stumbles on, like a drunken person. Sometimes he loses an arm, or an eye rolls out of his head, but the film zombie is not bothered. As long as he can take a bite out of a tasty arm or leg, he is happy. Only a shot right between the eyes can stop him. Only then does the zombie lie down for good.

Real zombies

In Haiti there are many stories about corpses that are dug up to be put to work on plantations. They are used as a form of slave labour. They are a cheap labour force and they never complain, because zombies can't hear, say or think anything.

A true zombie story. Imagine one day your neighbour, who died and was buried twenty years ago, walks into your living room. You would probably not believe your own eyes. And yet these things happen!

On 3rd May 1962, Clairvius Narcisse, a Haitian farmer, was buried in a graveyard north of his village, called l'Estère. Eighteen years later, in 1980, the very same Clairvius walked into the marketplace in l'Estère, as cool as a cucumber. He told everyone he had been the victim of voodoo. He had been changed into a zombie by a sorcerer his brother had hired. Clairvius had argued with his brother about an inheritance before he died and was buried. After his funeral, they had taken him from his grave and put him to work as a slave, together with other zombies. After two years, he managed to escape and spent the next sixteen years travelling across the island.

The curious thing was that this zombie could talk and tell people exactly what had happened. Normally zombies can't talk and they don't remember anything.

But Clairvius Narcisse even remembered his own funeral. He had a scar on his face from where a nail had hit him when they hammered the lid of the coffin shut.

In 1981 the BBC made a documentary about the case. The death certificate, the funeral arrangements, everything matched Clairvius's story. He had been officially declared dead and was buried. And yet there he was, walking around alive and well.

There are more cases like this in Haiti. People return years after their funeral. They can't tell exactly what happened, like Clairvius Narcisse. They have no memory and they have no soul. They walk around as if they were empty on the inside. In the psychiatric hospital in Port-au-Prince, Haiti's capital, there are a number of people who have become zombies. They don't talk and just stare into space. They don't appear to have any feelings at all. Sometimes their eyes turn in their sockets, so you can only see the whites of their eyes.

The biggest fear of many Haitians is not meeting a zombie, but turning into one. But why do people turn into zombies? And how? It is obvious that no one *wants* to become one of the walking dead. Zombies are made! And not by some factory in China. The zombie is one of the mysteries of voodoo.

What is voodoo?

Voodoo is a mysterious religion where complicated rituals, dances and trance play an important role. A trance is a state in which you are only half conscious, like in a dream. You can enter into a trance by dancing. During a voodoo ritual people often sacrifice animals. They slaughter goats and chickens and offer them to the gods.

Voodoo is originally from Africa. In the seventeenth century, African slaves brought their religion with them to Haiti. There, voodoo was mixed with the Catholic faith and the belief in supernatural things.

Black magic. Magic plays an important part in voodoo, both white magic (the power to heal) and black magic (the power to curse and put a spell on people). Just like witchcraft, voodoo uses dolls to put spells on people.

Possessed. In voodoo ceremonies it happens regularly that the people who are dancing enter into a trance and are possessed by spirits that get inside them and take control over them. They stop seeing and feeling anything. They walk on hot coals or broken glass with their bare feet without feeling pain.

Zombie makers

Each village in Haiti has a secret society, a small group of important people who protect the community. Both men and women can join. They are selected by other members of the secret society. The members get special passes and use secret passwords. Each secret society has its own voodoo priest, the *bokor*. A *bokor* is a sorcerer or witch doctor. If someone in the village breaks the law and causes trouble, they warn him and he is asked to leave. If he doesn't leave of his own free will, the *bokor* will turn him into a zombie. In that case it is a form of punishment. But there are also *bokors* who are happy to change someone into a zombie for money.

How do you make a zombie? According to the stories they tell in Haiti, a witch doctor has to do the following things to turn someone into a zombie. First he rides, sitting backwards on a horse, to the victim's house. When he is at the door, he puts his lips to the keyhole and sucks the victim's soul out of the house and blows it into a bottle. That is a very special kind of magic, and only a witch doctor can do this. He immediately puts a cork on the bottle. Now he has captured the victim's soul. The victim gets sick and dies. After the funeral, they take the corpse from the grave and bring it back to life using certain rituals. The witch doctor calls out his name, and the dead person opens his eyes and gets up. From now on, he is the witch doctor's slave, because the witch doctor has his soul. He has become one of the walking dead with no will of his own.

Zombie powder. To change someone into a zombie, the witch doctor can also use the notorious zombie powder. Zombie powder contains, among other things, ground-up plants, dried toads and crushed human bones.

The witch doctor scatters the zombie powder on the victim's doorstep, and when the victim steps on it, the powder enters his body through the soles of his feet. He dies and becomes a zombie.

Not actually dead. Making a zombie is pure witch-craft, no doubt about that. But Western researchers have been trying for years to come up with a different explanation for zombies. And at last they have found one: zombies aren't really dead when they are buried, they only *appear* to be dead. It looks as if they are dead, but they are actually still alive.

There are poisons that make a person appear dead. One of them is the poison of the puffer fish, a kind of fish you can find almost everywhere in the tropics. In 1982 the American professor Wade Davis discovered that puffer-fish poison is used in zombie powder. That means that a zombie is someone who was still alive when they were buried. Because of the zombie powder, the victim only appears to be dead. He is in a trance from which he will probably never wake again. When they pull him from the grave, he is a creature with no will – almost literally one of the walking dead.

Voodoo as amusement

Even though most Haitians have a deep-seated fear of the dark side of voodoo, they have started to organize voodoo spectacles for tourists. They show how black magic works and walk over hot coals and broken glass. They have parades in which people dress up and paint their faces deathly white, marching through the streets like zombies.

Bombie the Zombie

Zombies are very popular in films, but less so in books, and there are hardly any children's book about them. Could it be that zombies are too grim for children? Then again, there *are* some comic strips about zombies.

None other than Donald Duck had a scary adventure with a zombie. In the story 'Voodoo Hoodoo' from 1949, Donald meets one of the walking dead called Bombie the Zombie, who has been wandering the earth for seventy years. He gives Donald a voodoo doll, thinking he is his Uncle Scrooge. Donald accidentally pricks himself with a poisoned needle and

is cursed with the shrinking curse. He must travel
to Africa to find the witch doctor responsible for
the curse, the zombie's master. Only *he* can undo
the curse.

Salt against zombies

If you are scared of zombies, make sure you always have
some salt on you. When a zombie tastes salt, he wakes
up from his trance. He realizes he is actually dead and
will return to his grave.

6
Witches

Real witches wear ordinary clothes and look very much like ordinary women. They live in ordinary houses and work in ordinary jobs. That is why they are so hard to catch.

From *The Witches*, by Roald Dahl

The witch is the odd one out in this collection of creeps. She is not a monster or a supernatural being, but a human being. Witches really exist. At least, there have always been people who claim they are witches. Even now. Witches belong to the real world as well as an "alternative reality".

Throughout the ages, witches have been loved as well as hated. There are good witches and evil witches. Good witches help people, for example by making them better. Evil witches, though, make people ill.

People have written more history books about witches than horror stories. And yet witchcraft plays an important part in some scary stories and fairy tales. That is why the witch deserves a place in this book.

Witches can be male or female, but in stories, witches are nearly always women. Male witches are usually called sorcerers or wizards.

What is a witch?

Witches in fairy tales and children's stories. Evil witches, like the ones you find in fairy tales and children's stories, are ugly old women with warts and long, hooked noses who fly around on broomsticks and practise black magic. They live in little huts in the forest, and

every now and again they like to roast a child in the oven or hand out poisoned apples. Just think about the witches in 'Hansel and Gretel', 'Snow White' or *The Wonderful Wizard of Oz*. There are usually a couple of black cats or ravens lurking about too. Witches brew their magic potion in big cauldrons that have toads, toadstools, eyes, bits of hair and other yummy bits floating around in them.

Modern witches. Modern witches, like the ones Roald Dahl describes in his book *The Witches* (1983), are not ugly old hags. Instead, they look like nice ladies, but underneath their wigs, they are bald and scaly. When they take off their gloves, they have curvy claws. They don't have toes either, and their spit is blue. They are pure evil and hate all children.

But there are also good witches, as in Margaret Mahy's book *The Changeover* (1984). Three very special witches – grandmother, mother and son – help the main character Laura become a real witch. That way she can fight the demon that has taken control of her little brother.

Actual witches

There is a difference between the evil witch from fairy tales and scary stories and the actual witch we can read about in history books. Witchcraft goes back a long way and had been around long before people started telling stories about witches. And those ancient witches didn't look a bit like the evil witches you find in fairy tales.

Wise woman. In prehistoric times, witches were priestesses and healers who were known as wise women. They were honoured and treated with great respect, because they had magic powers. They also knew a lot about herbs that could cure people. By means of magic spells and rituals, they could get rid of enemies, or so people believed. But witches were also feared by their own people, because they were thought to communicate with the dead and the world of spirits.

Herbal healing. In the Middle Ages a witch was normally an old woman who knew a lot about herbs. Because there were so few doctors, people who were ill would often go to a witch for help. With herbal potions she could make sick people better. Witches were usually very poor. They lived in shabby houses and made a living from healing people and telling their fortunes. Even though people would go to witches for advice and help, they were afraid of their knowledge. It was these herbal healers that would later become the model for fairy-tale witches.

How do you become a witch?

Someone with a talent for witchcraft can be trained by a real witch or sorcerer and learn the secret arts of witchcraft. Old witches often had young people helping them. They would do household chores and learn all about the witching trade at the same time. In Otfried Preussler's *Krabat & the Sorcerer's Mill* (1971), the main character Krabat works in a mill, which turns out to be a kind of school for wizards. The miller is a master sorcerer who instructs his twelve pupils in the dark arts.

In Anthony Horowitz's *Groosham Grange* (1988) and in J.K. Rowling's *Harry Potter* novels (1997–2007), it appears that there are special boarding schools for witches and wizards nowadays.

The dark arts

Magic. Witches used magic. They could change people into toads or pigs with a magic spell or a potion. By "reading" the innards of a slaughtered chicken, they could predict the future.

Woe to you if you accepted a witch's invitation to come in for a cup of tea. The worst things imaginable could happen. You could shrink, shrivel up with old age, go doolally, turn into an animal and other such jolly things.

Flying around. Witches could fly on broomsticks. They normally left their house via the chimney, with a broomstick in between their legs. They sometimes used a kind of flying ointment they spread on their entire body. Nowadays people think that witches could not actually fly at all, but that the magic ointment they used made them *dream* they could fly. When they woke up, they were convinced they had really been flying hither and thither.

Creating storms. The broomstick was a powerful weapon for the witch. Not only could she use it to fly on, but by striking it very hard on the ground, she could cause storms, for example. They also thought that witches could create storms by throwing sand in the direction of the setting sun.

Conjuring up spirits. For a very, very long time people believed that witches were able to communicate with the world of spirits and the dead. Through mysterious rituals, they could conjure up evil spirits and give them orders to annoy other people. One of the most famous of these evil spirits was Astaroth, a hideous creature that was sometimes described as a cross between a cat, a toad, a spider and a human being.

Shape-shifting. Witches were able to change themselves and others into werewolves (see Chapter 3). They were also able to transform themselves into owls, ravens and other animals, just like a vampire.

Curses. With the help of a special doll, witches could put a curse on people. A curse is when you use special words that cause harm to other people. As a result, they can get sick or even die. The witch would stick something belonging to the person they wanted to curse to the doll: nail clippings, a few hairs or a fragment of their clothes. After that, she would utter her curse or stick needles in the doll. Even if the victim were miles away, they would suddenly start to hurt terribly. Sometimes they even died.

They do the same in voodoo, an African kind of witchcraft (see Chapter 5).

The evil eye. Witches could make awful things happen just by looking at you. They call this power "the evil eye". One look from the evil eye and that year's harvest would be destroyed, or all the milk would turn sour, just to give a few examples.

Some people still believe in the power of the evil eye. The belief is common in Ireland and Italy, among other places.

Protection against witches

Back when people were very afraid of witches, it was only natural that they looked for ways to protect themselves against the witchcraft. They made sure that witches couldn't come anywhere near them by wearing special necklaces, bracelets and all kinds of amulets, such as stones with holes in them.

Good witches. When people knew that an evil (black) witch had cursed them, they could go to a good (white) witch for help. She could undo the curse if she was powerful enough. She could make a witch's doll, for example, and so kill the evil witch.

Rowan tree. Up to the nineteenth century, the leaves or branches from the rowan tree were considered to protect you against the effects of black magic. They would hang crosses made from branches of the rowan tree above their doors to stop witches from coming in. They would also sometimes hang a rowan twig above a baby's cot. Necklaces made from rowanberries or blood coral also helped to scare off witches.

Garlic. It appears that garlic is not only an effective method to protect yourself against vampires, but people also believed it kept witches at a distance. By keeping a clove of garlic in your wallet or purse, you could be sure that a witch wouldn't stick her hand in to steal your money – because they also thought witches were great thieves.

Protection against the evil eye. To fend off a witch's evil eye, you had to hold up your index and little finger to form two horns (holding the other two fingers down with your thumb). You could also make the sign of the horn with your index and middle finger or with your little finger and your thumb. Another way of protecting your house against the evil eye was to paint an eye on it. And if you were very brave,  you could protect yourself by spitting three times in a witch's evil eye.

Witches' sabbaths

When witches got together, it was called a sabbath. They would do this four times a year. The most important meetings for witches were Walpurgis Night (the night between 30th April and 1st May) and Hallowe'en (the night between 31st October and 1st November). Ever since the Middle Ages, people have had the weirdest ideas about what took place at these witches' sabbaths. Because normal people were never at these meetings, the stories just got stranger and stranger in the course of the centuries. Stories about witches hanging out with the Devil spread as quickly then as rumours about Justin Bieber's latest girlfriend now.

In the sixteenth and seventeenth centuries this is what people believed happened at a witches' sabbath. On the eve of Walpurgis Night, witches from all corners of the earth would gather on a mountain or in a forest.

They would travel on broomsticks or on the back of a werewolf. Like Hallowe'en, Walpurgis Night is a dodgy time, when all sorts of spirits and demons are on the loose. The perfect night for a wild witches' party, then, with witches singing songs and gorging themselves on food. The witches would dance in a circle, wearing animal masks that were supposed to represent the Devil (bulls, stags and so forth). The mountain or the forest would be teeming with snakes, black cats, owls and bats. Demons would dance hand in hand with witches. In the moonlight you could see strange vapours rising from the cauldrons they used to prepare their feast. The witches would brag to each other about the evil things they had been up to, and together they planned more wicked deeds. When the party was in full swing, the Devil himself would arrive and check if the witches had been nasty enough. To show their obedience, the witches would kiss the Devil's backside.

When the party was over, the witches would get onto their broomsticks or werewolves once more and travel back home.

In Anthony Horowitz's book *The Devil's Door-bell* (1986), a nuclear power plant is used for a witches' sabbath. The witches want to make the Devil appear by using nuclear energy.

The witch-hunt

Because of these wild stories about witches' sabbaths and the magical powers of the herbal healers, people got more and more afraid of witches. The Church told everyone that witches worshipped the Devil because they used magic, and according to the Church, anything to do with magic was the Devil's work. The Church was convinced that all witches, even good ones who made people better, were the Devil's servants.

Witch-hunts became widespread in the sixteenth and seventeenth centuries. During the same period – all over Europe, but especially in France – people accused of being werewolves were also being burnt. If you look at the reports from that period, you would think just about every next person was either a witch or a were-wolf. That is how afraid people were of them. People no longer trusted their own neighbours. Both men and women could be accused of witchcraft, but it was mainly women who were suspected of being witches. Maybe witches have been persecuted so much because men were always afraid of powerful women. As far as we know, witch-hunters were always men.

Witch-hunters. The Church used informers, witch-hunters and a religious tribunal to capture, try and condemn any suspects of witchcraft. If a suspect didn't want to confess, he or she was tortured until they con-fessed that they were in fact a witch or a sorcerer. To help them achieve this, they would use thumbscrews and hot iron pokers. Another method they used was to roast parts of your body. Nice.

The swimming of witches. A famous test to see if you were suspected of witchcraft was called "swim-ming the witch". They tied the hands and feet of the presumed witch and threw her into the water. If she drowned, it proved she was not a witch. If she floated, she was a witch, and she would be burnt at the stake or hanged, depending on which country she happened to be tried in.

Warts, moles and freckles. It didn't take long before people were more afraid of witch-hunters than they were of witches. Anyone could be accused of being a witch. Especially people with the following marks on their bodies ran a great risk: a scar on your eyebrow, a mole in your neck, a freckle under your hair, a wart on your ear, a slightly different colour in part of your eye or a cleft chin.

At a trial for witchcraft any of these marks could get you convicted, and you would be condemned to death, because the Church believed they were the Devil's marks.

Witch-pricking needles. When a witch-hunter couldn't find anything in the face of a suspect, she had to take off her clothes and they would look all over her body for moles or other marks of the Devil. To find these marks they used special witch-pricking needles to stab the witch with. If she happened not to feel anything when she was pricked, it meant she was a witch. The strange thing is that a number of victims didn't deny the accusations. Right up to the moment they were burnt at the stake, they insisted they were real witches.

Matthew Hopkins. One of the most notorious witch-hunters was Matthew Hopkins. He would travel through East Anglia, going from town to town, putting witches to death and drowning them. Together with his colleague John Stearne, he killed more witches than all other English witch-hunters put together. According to some stories, he died of tuberculosis, but some say his own neighbours drowned him because they were fed up to the back teeth with his cruelty. If that is true, he died the same way many witches did when they had to do the swimming test. In 1968 there was a horror film made about Hopkins called *Witchfinder General*.

Salem Witch Trials. The most famous witch trials in history were the ones held in Salem, Massachusetts, and nearby towns between February 1692 and May 1693. It all began when the daughter and niece of the local Puritan minister, aged nine and eleven, started to behave as if they were possessed by the Devil. They accused some people in the neighbourhood of being witches, and a court was created in Salem to hear the witnesses and the accused. Soon many more people, especially women, were involved in the trial and condemned to death. Twenty people – fourteen of them women – were executed, and five died in prison, including two infants. It was later discovered that the trials were all based on false accusations and panic spreading among the population. This sad episode was the subject of a famous play called *The Crucible* (1953) by Arthur Miller and of a film of the same title, released in 1996.

People seriously believed in witches. One of the reasons behind the Salem witch trials was that most people did believe that witches existed and were dangerous creatures – some still believe it today! King James I of England wrote a treatise on demons and witchcraft called *Demonology* (1597), showing that even kings and queens seriously believed in these things. In this book he also mentions "war-woolfes", that is to say "werewolves" (see Chapter 3).

The end of the "witch craze". At the end of the seventeenth century people were no longer so keen on spilling witches' blood. But it wasn't until the eighteenth century – with some cases even later than that – that witchcraft trials came to an end. New laws were made and witchcraft was now seen as superstitious nonsense. But before then, tens of thousands of people in England, Germany, France, Spain, Italy and other countries were killed because they were believed to be witches. The story about the witch craze is more horrific than any other horror story – because it actually happened.

Witches today

Witches in the English language. Despite the horrific stories from the past, witches live on in the English language. We still refer to old, ugly women as witches or hags ("hag" is related to the German word for witch, "*Hexe*"). We can also feel "bewitched". In fact, this can be a very positive thing, like in the song 'Bewitched, Bothered and Bewildered' (recorded by many artists, including Rod Stewart and Cher in 2006). It is interesting to note that even love is often linked to magic: we can be "enchanted", "charmed" and "fascinated" (this word is originally linked to the "evil eye").

The witch lives on, both in our language and in real life.

Covens. All over the world, modern witches meet in covens. These are clubs for witches. They often have thirteen members because 13 is a magic number for them. Some of its members see themselves as great-great-grandchildren of the witches from the past. They organize ancient rituals and hold mysterious meetings. They are people you meet every day: housewives, teachers, headmasters, bank clerks, writers, artists and scientists. Perfectly ordinary people, then. Although…

Perfectly ordinary? What does Roald Dahl say again in his book *The Witches*? "REAL WITCHES wear ordinary clothes and look very much like ordinary women. They live in ordinary houses and work in ORDINARY JOBS. That is why they are so hard to catch."

These witches only have one goal: to exterminate all children. They have a special nose for children. They can sniff them out even when they are miles away.

The more you wash yourself, the better they can smell you.

So there is only one way to escape their attention: never take a bath ever again!

They use the same method in the East. Parents believe that they can protect their children against the evil eye by allowing them to get really dirty. That is because the witch will only point her evil eye at children who are scrubbed clean. But how do you convince your parents of that?…

7

Monsters

He'd also gathered about himself an army of nearly every evil creature imaginable: dragons, trolls, goblins - and, most terrifying of all, the Black Fairy.

From *Alistair Grim's Odd Aquaticum*, by Gregory Funaro

The word "monster" is defined by the *Oxford English Dictionary* in this way: "Originally: a mythical creature which is part animal and part human, or combines elements of two or more animal forms, and is frequently of great size and ferocious appearance. Later, more generally: any imaginary creature that is large, ugly, and frightening."

Most monster belong to the "alternative reality". But there are real monsters too. They live in the depths of our oceans, lakes and lochs, and on snowy mountain tops, or in jungles where no humans have set foot.

So hop on board the monster bus and get ready for a short tour during which you will meet monsters past and present.

Frankenstein's monster

Frankenstein's monster is scary, big and ugly. He was made in a laboratory by a certain Doctor Frankenstein. This monster is a huge creature with a square skull, a forehead shaped like a brick and two large bolts sticking out of his neck. It was the actor Boris Karloff who made him famous. He played the role of Frankenstein's monster in the film *Frankenstein* (1931). People often think that Frankenstein is the name of the monster, but that is not true. Frankenstein is the name of his creator, Doctor Viktor Frankenstein. The monster itself has no name. As mentioned before, the book *Frankenstein* was written in 1818 by Mary Shelley, and her monster is still as popular as ever. The name Frankenstein has become legendary, even for those who have not seen the film or read the book. They even use the name Frankenstein to insult people. You can also buy plastic monster assembly kits that allow you to build your own Frankenstein's monster.

You can read more about *Frankenstein* in Chapters 8 and 9.

Blubbery mass. Another monster that was created in a laboratory is described in Vivian Alcock's *The Monster Garden* (1988, 2000), where the eleven-year-old Frances Stein (pay attention to her name!) creates a monster in a dish from some kind of blubbery mass she has taken from her dad's laboratory.

Mummies

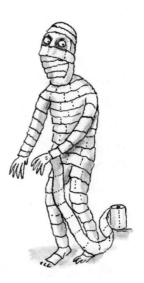

This is another human monster. The mummy is a monster you only really find in old horror films and comic strips. You don't read much about mummies in books. That is because all mummy stories are the same. The mummy from horror films and comic strips is a lot like the zombie. They are both walking corpses. The difference is that a mummy is very, very old and covered from head to toe in bandages.

Thousands of years ago the Ancient Egyptians wrapped dead people in linen. Before that, they would embalm the body. They would put the body in a special bath and rub it with special oils and ointments. When you treat a body this way, it doesn't rot away.

A mummy story is always about a mummified body that comes back to life after two or three thousand years, because someone broke into his tomb, for example, triggering an old curse. Unfortunately, after so many centuries of being dead, the mummy wakes up stark raving mad. He leaves his tomb and murders everyone who crosses his path. Underneath the bandages, he is nothing more than a skeleton covered in a shrivelled-up skin. After thousands of years, his body has not rotted away, but it has become all dried up. His movements are wooden and stiff, just like a zombie's.

In the film *The Mummy* (1944), a mummy that is thousands of years old tries to kidnap a girl because he thinks she is his wife. Needless to say, the girl is not very chuffed.

King Kong

The first time people saw King Kong was in a film from 1933. He is a giant gorilla who lives on an island in the Indian Ocean. There he fights with prehistoric animals, which apparently haven't died out on the island. The people of the island worship him as a god. The giant gorilla is brought to New York by some American filmmakers who want to put him on display in a theatre where people have to pay a lot of money to see him. But King Kong escapes and creates a massive chaos. Meanwhile, he falls in love with a film star and, clutching her in his paw, climbs up the Empire State Building, the world's highest building at the time. In the end he is shot down by airplanes and dies.

Most horror fans feel sorry for King Kong and have to wipe away a little tear when he dies. Strangely enough, the monster from the 1933 film is nicer than the people. Even today, King Kong remains one of the most popular monsters ever. In shops they sell King Kong dolls, assembly kits, comic strips, mechanical toys and even video games, including *Donkey Kong*, in which he appears as the villain, chased and ultimately floored by Mario of *Super Mario Bros.* fame. After the original film (remade by Peter Jackson in 2005), many other films about gigantic apes were made, such as *Son of Kong* (1933) and *Mighty Joe Young* (1949). But no other gorilla is as famous as King Kong. Just as with Frankenstein's monster, even if you haven't seen the film, you know who King Kong is. He is a legend among horror fans.

Monstrous spiders

Apart from being afraid of large predators like tigers, crocodiles and sharks, many people are afraid of one particular small creature: the spider. Filmmakers and writers use this fear to their advantage. There are countless films about monster spiders, like *Tarantula* (1953) and *Arachnophobia* (1990). You can read more about these films in Chapter 8.

Huge spiders crawl out of the pages of some books too. In Tim Curran's *The Underdwelling* (2012), when a search party is trapped underground, they meet a monstrous spidery creature that had lived there undisturbed for centuries. The giant spider Shelob, who threatens Frodo and Sam in *The Lord of the Rings* (1954–55), is very scary too. In this masterpiece by the English writer J.R.R. Tolkien – famously adapted into a series of three films by Peter Jackson between 2001 and 2003 – the hobbits Frodo and Sam, peace-loving creatures with hair on their feet, have to battle with trolls, dragons, ring wraiths and countless other monsters to destroy a dangerous magical ring.

Greek monsters

In Greek myths (stories the ancient Greeks told about their gods and heroes) you come across a whole range of monsters. There were monsters who were part human, but others were one hundred per cent animal. Their main function was to be killed by the hero of the story.

Cerberus. The Greeks believed that after you died you would go to the underworld, which they called Hades. The entrance to this realm of the dead was guarded by Cerberus, the Hound of Hell. Cerberus was the kind of dog that would scare even a pit bull terrier out of its wits. It had three monstrous heads and three snake-like tails. Cerberus made sure no living being could enter the underworld, or a dead person sneak out.

Medusa. Medusa was the youngest of three monstrous sisters called the Gorgons. Instead of hair, she had snakes growing out of her head. She also had fangs and wings. Medusa was the most dangerous of the three sisters. If you looked her in the eye, you would not be able to tell the tale, because you would be turned to stone. It was the hero Perseus who cut off Medusa's head. Instead of looking at her directly, he looked at her reflection in his shiny shield and decapitated her. Later, he cleverly used her head to defeat a dragon. He made the dragon look into Medusa's dead eyes. As a result the dragon turned to stone.

Cyclopes. Cyclopes were colossal giants who only had one eye in the middle of their forehead. They were so huge they could pile one mountain on top of the other, as if they were pieces of Lego. They were ogres, or man-eating giants. One of them was called Polyphemus, who got on the wrong side of the famous Greek hero Odysseus at one point.

Harpies. Harpies were monsters that were half woman, half bird, with claws on their hands and feet. They liked nothing better than to torment humans. They were also known as storm birds because they would dive out of the sky like thun-derbolts and rob everything that came in their path, like a storm. Whatever was left behind they covered in bird poo.

Zeus, the ruler of the gods, called them his hounds. He would send them to attack human beings when he wanted to punish them for disobeying him.

Minotaur. King Minos of Crete built a huge labyrinth with hundreds of rooms and corridors in which he locked up the Minotaur. This monster was half human, half bull. He only ate human flesh, and if you got lost in the maze by mistake, he would be waiting for you with wide-open arms, and jaws!

Hydra. This monster was a water snake or water-dragon with no fewer than nine heads. It was nearly impossible to defeat, because as soon as you chopped off one head, two new ones would appear. The only way the hero Hercules managed to defeat it was with the help of his friend Iolaus. Whenever Hercules hacked off a head, Iolaus would immediately burn the stump with a burning piece of wood, making it impossible for the Hydra to grow new heads.

Dragons

According to some ancient stories, the dragon's ancestors were worms or snakes. That is why in the Middle Ages people thought that dragons lived in holes in the ground.

Western dragons are, without exception, fierce and frightening monsters. In most stories dragons look like oversized lizards with wings, or winged snakes with legs, breathing fire and smoke, burning everything in their path to a cinder. Dragons have one head or more – sometimes they even have dozens of heads. The number of feet also varies, ranging from two to six. The dragon's wings are like those of a bat. Its body is covered in scales, like a suit of armour, which makes it very hard to kill a dragon. It eats people and devours cattle. Elephants are its favourite dish.

One of the oldest descriptions of a dragon in English is in a poem written between 700 and 1000 AD that is usually referred to as *Beowulf*, although its original title and author are unknown. In it, the hero Beowulf first kills a horrible monster called Grendel, then its mother, only to be mortally wounded in the end by a nasty old dragon.

In Astrid Lindgren's *The Brothers Lionheart* (1973) there appears a huge and terrifying dragon called Katla. The dragon has to fight to the death with Karm, a gigantic, prehistoric monster snake.

Komodo dragon. There are real dragons that live on the Indonesian island of Komodo. The Komodo dragon was discovered in 1912 when an airplane had to make an emergency landing on the island. This is not a fire-breathing dragon and it doesn't have wings. It doesn't eat elephants but deer, which it kills by sneaking up on them. With its jaws it breaks the deer's neck and then gobbles it up. The Komodo dragon can reach more than three metres in length. Yikes.

Dragon and their hoards. Dragons hate people and hoard treasures. In many stories they sleep on top of a mountain of gold and jewels, like the dragon Smaug in *The Hobbit* by J.R.R. Tolkien (1937). Dragons are light sleepers. As soon as someone approaches their hoard, they are wide awake. Any thieves will be roasted immediately.

Dragon's blood. If you bathe in dragon blood, no one can beat you. Siegfried, a hero from Norse and German myths, became invincible after he killed the dragon Fafnir and had taken a bath in its blood. He could even understand the language of birds after drinking some of the dragon's blood.

For witches, dragon's blood is a powerful ingredient, which they often use in their magic potions.

Friendly dragons. There is a clear difference between Eastern and Western dragons. Eastern dragons, for instance in Chinese and Japanese stories, are usually good-natured, even though they look like real dragons. They bring happiness, and that is why in China the dragon is an important symbol. You can see dragons carved on the thrones of emperors, ships, beds, chairs, table legs and even coffins in China.

But there are examples of friendly dragons even in Western literature. One of them is Falkor, the white luckdragon from Michael Ende's *The Neverending Story* (1983). Another one is Toothless in Cressida Cowell's popular series of books (2003–15) on how to train a dragon and do a lot of other fun, dragonny things.

Actual monsters?

Even in our time there are many stories from all over the world about monsters. According to the film director Alfred Hitchcock, the twentieth century was the century of monsters. And even now they don't only roar and growl in films and cartoons, but they live in our oceans, lakes and lochs, and in remote jungles and on snowy mountains.

The Kraken. The Kraken is a legendary Norwegian sea monster, a kind of gigantic squid or octopus. Sailors in the fifteenth and sixteenth centuries were already telling stories about it. But even more recently than that, sailors have spotted giant squids lurking in our oceans that are true living nightmares. Whale-hunters who have seen them say they range from six to fifty metres in length. They also say that these monster drag whole whales with them into the depths of the ocean. The Kraken has two long ten-

tacles it uses to grab its prey, and eight tentacles with suckers to hold it down. With its parrot-like beak it rips its victim to shreds.

There is a very impressive version of the Kraken in the film 20,000 *Leagues under the Sea* (1954), based on a book by Jules Verne from 1870.

The Loch Ness Monster. The Loch Ness Monster, or "Nessie", is known throughout the world. But calling it a monster is no longer correct, because Nessie is loved more than she is feared. She is one of the very few monsters with a pet name.

Loch Ness is a loch in the Scottish mountains. It is twenty-three miles long and very deep. Since 1933, many people have taken countless photographs of Nessie. Unfortunately, none of them are very sharp or convincing. There is also a hazy film in which you see something massive coming out of the water. It seems certain that there is *something* in the waters of Loch Ness. But whether it is a sea snake, a prehistoric animal or something else, that is still not clear.

More water monsters. If Nessie really exists, she is not alone. Other countries have their water monsters too. In Canada they have a monster called Ogopogo, which lives in Lake Okanagan. It is a snake-like monster, more than twenty metres long, with a tail and flippers.

Manipogo is the name of another giant snake that swims about in Lake Manitoba and Lake Winnipegosis. It has its own little monster family, complete with wife and kids.

There have also been dozens of sightings of monsters in Ireland and Japan. They are usually described as gigantic snakes or like Plesiosauruses (prehistoric animals that lived 135 million years ago).

Yeti or the Abominable Snowman. People have been telling stories about the Abominable Snowman since 1832. It lives in the Himalayas, in Tibet. The Tibetans call it Yeti, which means "little man-like animal" according to the *Oxford English Dictionary* (even though it is supposed to be huge) – or it could be the Tibetan word for "rock bear" or just "bear". No one really knows. Every now and again, a short article will appear, tucked away in a corner of a newspaper, saying that some massive footprints have been seen on the snowy slopes of the Himalayas. These footprints are the only proof that the Yeti actually exists. But they are quite something. Some of them are half a metre long. Like Nessie, this monster has been spotted by many people. Most of them describe the Yeti as an ape-like creature, between eight and thirteen feet tall. It has a red fur and its skull looks like half a coconut. Local mountain guides claim its tracks point backwards. The Yeti is incredibly strong and can uproot trees.

The famous mountaineer Sir Edmund Hillary discovered huge footprints in the snow when he climbed Mount Everest in 1953. In 1961 he organized an expedition to find the Yeti. The only thing he brought back with him was a skull, which might belong to the Abominable Snowman. But Sir Edmund Hillary never found the Yeti itself.

If you want to have a good idea about the Yeti, you should read Hergé's *Tintin in Tibet* (1962).

Bigfoot. The Abominable Snowman has a relative in North America. In the States they call him Bigfoot, and in Canada he is known as Sasquatch. These cousins of the Yeti make it difficult for researchers too, because like the Abominable Snowman, they only ever leave footprints. But it is these footprints that make Bigfoot and the Abominable Snowman so mysterious. Imagine coming across some inexplicable footprints in your backyard. You would want to know who or what made them, especially if whatever made them is a size 21!

Extraterrestrial Monsters

BEM. For the time being, we don't have to be afraid that monsters will die out. There are plenty of new monsters out there in space, ready to come and pay us a visit.

Extraterrestrial monsters live on other planets. You see them mostly in science-fiction films. They have only been around for a little more than one hundred years. In the first half of the twentieth century, they called them BEM: bug-eyed monsters. They looked like octopuses or giant insects and had eyes on stalks. They would come to earth to steal women or conquer the world. The most famous BEM story is *The War of the Worlds* by H.G. Wells from 1897. In this story earth is attacked by Martians that look like enormous jellyfish.

In 1938 the actor and film director Orson Welles made a radio play based on the book which became very famous. During the broadcast of the radio play, people in America panicked. The radio play sounded so real and convincing that many Americans thought their country was actually under attack from extraterrestrial monsters. The book was first adapted into a film in 1953, and then remade more recently (2005) by Stephen Spielberg, with Tom Cruise starring as the man who is fighting for the survival of humankind after the deadly Martian invasion.

Aliens. Nowadays extraterrestrials are often called "aliens". With the exception of E.T., the cute extraterrestrial in Steven Spielberg's film from 1982, most aliens are still out to get us. I can hear the horror fan breathe a sigh of relief. "Phew! Otherwise things would get rather boring around here."

In the scary science-fiction film *Alien* (1979), an extraterrestrial monster brutally slaughters everyone on board a spaceship. The film was so successful that three sequels and a prequel were made (see Chapter 8).

All sorts of aliens pack the pages of Richard Moses's collection of humorous poems about our "frenemies" from space, *Aliens Stole My Underpants* (1998).

Cruel, hideous and repulsive monsters

The finish off this chapter we need to mention one more monster. It is described in Fredric Brown's short story *Sentry* (1954).

The story is told by someone who lands on a strange planet with his spaceship. He discovers that the planet has been conquered by the "enemy". The enemy is a race of cruel, hideous and repulsive monsters that wage war without negotiations or peace talks. Just looking at them makes him feel sick. He will never get used to them, he says. They are revolting creatures "with only two arms and two legs, ghastly white skins and no scales".

You have guessed it! They are humans!

8
Horror Films

(by Eddy C. Bertin)

Listen to them, the children of the night. What music
they make!

Bela Lugosi in the film *Dracula* (1931)

There are thousands of horror films for adults and
hardly any for children. Some films are terrific, others
truly horrible. Some are so bad, they make you laugh.
Of those thousands of films, I will only discuss the
best... and the worst. But I need to warn you: most
films are not for children, and you should not watch
them alone.

Enjoy your meal!

Everyone likes tasty food. But in films, you can get a
nasty surprise sometimes. Do you remember the soup
Indiana Jones is served in *Indiana Jones and the Temple*

of Doom (1984)? It has lots of eyes floating around in it. In *The Hitcher* (1986), the main character, a young man, orders some chips and, as he is munching away, he discovers he is chewing on a severed finger. In the atrociously bad film *Blood Diner* (1987), two crazy brothers put human meat in their spaghetti sauce. In the comedy *How to Eat Fried Worms* (2006), a boy with a queasy stomach is bullied into eating ten worms in one day or face horrible consequences. Things get funnier when food is trying to eat *you*. That is what happens in *The Stuff* (1985), where a new kind of ice cream makes your tummy swell up and eats you up from the inside.

Can I offer you a glass of blood?

Now that I have mentioned food, how about a drink? No, I am not talking about a glass of water, but a little bit of blood straight from the artery. Nice and warm and syrupy. That is of course what vampires specialize in. One of the oldest horror movies is a vampire film called *Nosferatu* (1922). (The name "nosferatu", as we have seen before, means "undead".) The vampire, whose name is Orlok, is played by an actor who

called himself Max Schreck. He had chosen a good name, because Schreck in German means "fright". It is a silent film, and when it was originally shown, they had someone playing along on the piano in the auditorium.

The story is entirely based on Bram Stoker's *Dracula*. That is why Bram Stoker's heirs took the filmmaker to court and demanded they destroy all copies of the film. Fortunately some copies survived.

The vampire in the film is long and thin and wears a black cape. He is bald and his bat-like ears stick out of his head. He has bulging eyes and long, thin fingers with very long nails. His long, pointy vampire fangs are in the front of his mouth, like a rabbit's teeth. That is what the first vampire fangs in film history looked like. Later, Klaus Kinski would play the role of Dracula with the same kind of fangs in *Nosferatu the Vampyre* (1979).

Hopping vampires

There are only a few other vampires that have these frontal fangs. Japanese vampires also have them. These appear in films like *The Jitters* (1989) and *Vampire Raiders: Ninja Queen* (1988). Japanese vampires are a bit different from the ones we are familiar with. They come out of their grave as stiff as a plank that you put upright. They wear kimonos and hop around like rabbits! To destroy them, you must stick magic words written on a bit of silk to their forehead. When you do that, they stop hopping about and you can cut off their head. They are a scream.

The origin of the classic vampire fangs

"Our" vampires have long, pointy canine teeth. This tradition goes back to the theatre. At the end of the nineteenth century and the beginning of the twentieth, a number of vampire plays were put on. You can imagine it must have been tough to speak for an actor with those huge fangs stuck to his front teeth. That is why they gave them long canine teeth instead. That way, they could speak in a way that people could understand (although it still needs a bit of practice). When they started making vampire films, they continued the tradition, and vampires ended up having long canine teeth.

Dracula, the king of the vampires

Bela Lugosi played the first true Dracula in the film *Dracula* (1931). Lugosi's real name was Béla Blaskó and he was from Hungary. He had been an actor since 1901. He moved to America and became famous because of his role as a vampire. He also played in many other horror films. It all went to his head, though, and he began to dress as Dracula in real life, wearing black capes and massive rings. He even slept in a coffin and was eventually buried in his vampire cape.

In most old black-and-white films, vampires don't have fangs. The first time you see vampire fangs is when Christopher Lee played the Count in *Horror of Dracula* (1958). His enemy, Doctor van Helsing, was played by Peter Cushing. Originally Christopher Lee was called Christopher Carradini, and his family was Italian. Before he became an actor, he was an opera singer. He played in many horror films: as a mummy, as Mr Hyde, as Fu Manchu and even as Frankenstein's monster. Lee was terrific as Dracula: he was tall and had a thin, noble face. He didn't have to speak much, but he said it all with his fangs and his red, blood-shot eyes (lenses, really). He played the role in seven films, but more and more reluctantly. He was tired of only ever being cast as a vampire. The last Dracula film he played in is hilarious: *Dracula and Son* (1976). In it, Dracula has to make a TV ad for toothpaste to make a living. The most recent Dracula films are Francis Ford Coppola's *Bram Stoker's Dracula* (1992), an impressive, bloody spectacle with a great soundtrack, and Stephen Sommers's *Van Helsing* (2004).

Mind if we take a bite?

There are tons of vampire films that are scary and funny at the same time. In *Love at First Bite* (1976), the vampire is a disco-dancing playboy. In *Fright Night* (1985) a teenage boy gets a new neighbour who turns out to be a vampire, but no one believes him. In *The Lost Boys* (1987) too, it is the kids who take on the punk vampires, using what they learnt from reading comic strips. In *The Fearless Vampire Killers* aka *Dance of the Vampires* (1967), the main character avoids being bitten by stuffing a Bible into the vampire's mouth just as he is opening his jaws wide. There is even a vampire dog called Zoltan, as you can see in *Zoltan, Hound of Dracula* aka *Dracula's Dog* (1978). It has vampire fangs and its eyes light up red.

It's alive, it's alive!

Frankenstein is the name of a scientist who creates a monster from various bits of corpses. Peter Cushing played the role of Baron Frankenstein many times, but the monster is of course much more famous. The very first monster movie ever made was *Frankenstein,* and it was filmed in 1910. The film only lasted ten minutes and all that is left is some photographs.

In 1931 the English actor William Henry Pratt, better known as Boris Karloff, shot to fame in his role as the monster. When Bela Lugosi no longer wanted to play the role, it was offered to Boris Karloff, who ended up playing the monster in *Frankenstein* (1931) and a number of sequels. With his large body, his deep-set eyes and the make-up that made his face look square, he really was a horrific monster. After the success of the first film, they made *The Bride of Frankenstein* (1935) and *Son of Frankenstein* (1939). All in all, Karloff played in about one hundred horror films.

A number of years later, they made another series of Frankenstein films. Christopher Lee played the monster in *The Curse of Frankenstein* (1957). A more recent film *Frankenstein: The College Years* (1991) is nothing but a series of silly jokes. The latest adaptation is a science-fiction fantasy horror called *Victor Frankenstein* (2015), starring Daniel Radcliffe of *Harry Potter* fame and James McAvoy.

The funniest film, though, is without a doubt *Young Frankenstein* (1974). In this film the monster doesn't have big bolts but a zip around his neck.

Who is that, howling at the moon?

There must be at least one hundred werewolf films. The scariest is *Curse of the Werewolf* (1961), in which Oliver Reed transforms into a werewolf in a truly horrendous way. The film stresses that he doesn't *want* to change into a werewolf, but there is nothing he can do about it. *Wolves* (1981) is scary too, because you see everything from the werewolf's point of view.

The most impressive scenes are when you actually see someone's face change into a wolf's snout. This happens in *An American Werewolf in London* (1981) and *The Howling* (1980). In both films you get a lot of horror and gore, but there are also some funny scenes.

More recent films are the slightly absurd and action-packed *Skin Walkers* (2006) and *Red Riding Hood* (2011), a weird crossover between a horror movie and the classic fairy tale that you can find in Perrault and the brothers Grimm.

Other classic film monsters

There are a couple of other monsters that keep reappearing in old and new films. A good example is *The Phantom of the Opera* (1925). The role was first played by Lon Chaney Jr. The story is about a man with a horrifically burnt face who hides in the basement of the Paris Opera. There are several films about the phantom – including one made in 2004 – as well as a musical that has been playing in the West End for thirty years and is available on DVD: *The Phantom of the Opera at the Royal Albert Hall*.

The story of *Dr Jekyll and Mr Hyde* has been filmed many times too, with Anthony Perkins, Michael Caine and other famous actors starring in the leading role.

Other horror classics include films about waxworks museums where murder victims are displayed as dummies. The first of these films was called *Mystery of the Wax Museum* (1933), but the scariest is no doubt *House of Wax* (1953), in which Vincent Price plays the role of the crazy artist. Vincent Price was an American actor well known for his roles as baddy in a whole range of excellent horror films. Another version of the story is *Waxwork* (1988), in which the visitors to a waxworks museum enter into another world via the figures on display. Once they are on "the other side", vampires and werewolves are waiting for them.

Films about mummies have become a little old-fashioned. They all tell the same story: tomb raiders enter a pyramid protected by an ancient curse, then a mummy wakes up and starts killing people. The best of these films are both simply called *The Mummy*, one with Boris Karloff from 1932, and another with Christopher Lee from 1959.

Anyone interested in huge dragons?

Everyone likes dinosaurs. In *The Beast from 20,000 Fathoms* (1953), nuclear explosions wake up a dinosaur that had been frozen in ice for millions of years. In *Dinosaurus!* (1960) a man-eating monster comes alive, and is defeated in the end with the help of a crane.

In *Gorgo!* (1961), one of these dragon-like monsters is captured and put on display in a circus. But it turns out the monster is only a baby, and its mother comes to the rescue! Mummy dragon is as tall as a tower and razes London to the ground.

A whole series of films were made in Japan about Godzilla, a dinosaur created by nuclear explosions. Godzilla breathes fire and fights a number of other monsters. In most films, this turns into a tussle in which entire cities are destroyed. The Godzilla brand has since spread to Western audiences, with Godzilla films made in 1998 and 2014.

But the most successful dinosaur film franchise is the one based on Michael Crichton's novels *Jurassic Park* (1990) and *The Lost World* (1995). They have proved so popular that a further two film sequels have come out.

Monster from outer space

Even an extraterrestrial monster like the one in *Alien* (1979) looks a bit like a dinosaur, except it has a double mouth full of sharp teeth. This monster terrorizes the crew of a spaceship. One of the most horrific scenes is when the monster bursts out of the belly of one of the astronauts. The sequels *Aliens* (1986), *Alien 3* (1992) and *Alien: Resurrection* (1997) – as well as the 2012 prequel *Prometheus* – are just as gruesome. In fact, the theme of these films is not that original. It is the same story as *It! The Terror from beyond Space* (1958). And in *Dark Side of the Moon* (1989), none other than the Devil comes aboard a spaceship.

Sometimes, monsters from outer space land on earth. In *The Thing from Another World* (1951), scientists find a flying saucer at the North Pole. It is buried deep beneath the ice. They defrost the creature they find inside the UFO, which then tries to murder them by taking the shape of a human being. A later version called *The Thing* (1982) is pretty scary because of its special effects, but it has funny moments too. One of the funniest is when the creature hides in a cut-off head. The head grows legs and walks away like a massive spider.

Spiders and other creepy-crawlies

Most people are afraid of spiders, rats and snakes, or at least they dislike them. No wonder you see them all the time in horror films, where they make people's life hell. In *The Giant Spider Invasion* (1975), first the people are

threatened by a whole flock of normal-size tarantulas, then a giant spider appears. It has bright-red eyes and it is obvious that its legs are powered by a machine. Compared to that, the *Kingdom of Spiders* (1977) is much scarier. In that film the spiders take over the world. *Arachnophobia* (1990) is both funny and scary. It shows a pest-control guy attacking spiders like a cowboy, using spray guns instead of revolvers.

The first giant spider appeared in a film called *Tarantula* (1955). The monster was the result of experiments with nuclear energy. The same happens in *Them!* (1954) and *Empire of the Ants* (1977), in which the earth is threatened by humongous ants. There are also films with giant beetles, octopuses and much more. There is one massive spider we should not forget: the enormous monster in *It* (1990). In the end it gets killed by... a catapult.

There are many other horror films where animals attack humans. It is birds that attack people in Alfred Hitchcock's impressive film *The Birds* (1963). In *The Butterfly Murders* (1979) – you guessed it – it is butterflies. Apart from that, there are killer bees, bats, snakes, crocodiles, rats, cockroaches – you name it.

Real highlights are the killer frogs in *Frogs* (1972) or the rabbits in *The Night of the Lepus* (1972), where you have rabbits as big as cows attacking humans. Things can't get any weirder than that.

But let us not forget our dear pets. There are wild dogs in *The Pack* (1977) and furious cats in *The Uncanny* (1977) and *Strays* (1991). And what about a man who changes into a human-sized fly in *The Fly* (1958, 1986)?

Steel monsters

Monsters don't always have to be animal-like creatures. In horror films any everyday object can become a killer. In Stephen King's *Maximum Overdrive* (1986) electric knives and lawnmowers start attacking people. At the same time, cars all over the world are taken over by an evil power and they become the new rulers. This is a bit like *The Car* (1977), where a car is possessed by a demon and starts killing people. In *Christine* (1983) a ghost car is jealous of its owner. In Steven Spielberg's *The Duel* (1971), a tanker truck with a mysterious driver at the wheel chases a terrified motorist along the highway in the California desert.

Can I come and haunt your house, please?

Now that we have mentioned ghosts, there are tons and tons of haunted houses in horror films. In *The Haunting* (1963, remade in 1999) and *Legend of Hell House* (1973), scientists are trying to find out if the house is really haunted by ghosts… with hair-raising results.

In *The Nesting* (1981) and *Lady in White* (1988) old crimes are solved by ghosts. Other haunted houses turn out to be built on former graveyards, with the result that the dead cannot find peace. This is the case in *Poltergeist* (1982) and *Grave*  *Secrets* (1992). One of the most famous haunted houses is the one in *The Amityville Horror* (1979), where an entire family is driven out of their house by an evil spirit. This film, like *Grave Secrets*, is supposed to be based on a "true story" (if you are willing to believe that, of course). Both *Amityville Horror* and *Poltergeist* had many sequels, as you can imagine.

The dead are coming out of their graves

Apart from traditional ghosts and phantoms, there are walking dead or zombies. Two of the most famous old zombie films are *White Zombie* (1932) and *I Walked with a Zombie* (1943).

The first modern zombie film was *Night of the Living Dead* (1968). This film was shot in black-and-white by amateurs and is now world-famous. In this film zombies come out of their graves to feed on human flesh. They are real human-hunters. *Night of the*

Living Dead was so successful that it spawned five sequels and one prequel, each film more gruesome than the previous one. They really turn your stomach and make you lose your appetite. Then there is the horror comedy *The Return of the Living Dead* (1985) – also followed by a few sequels – which is scary and very funny at the same time. A zombie is chopped into bits, but it continues as if nothing has happened. Its head is rolling on the floor while its legs shuffle off somewhere else.

More recent series and films don't bother so much with corpses crawling out of their tombs. Instead, zombies are the result of a contagious disease. If you are bitten by a zombie, you become one yourself and start attacking other people. As you can imagine, things can easily get out of hand, and the world is in serious risk of being taken over by zombies or "walkers", as they are called in the popular series *The Walking Dead* (which started in 2010 and is still going). Something similar happens in the apocalyptic horror film *World War Z* (2013), starring Brad Pitt.

The kids will be OK

Many horror films have kids in them. They are often threatened, but usually they are able to stand up for themselves. In one of the most famous horror films of all time, *The Exorcist* (1973), a little girl is possessed by a real demon, which makes her do disgusting things. The little girl changes into a revolting little devil until a priest sacrifices himself to free her from the demon. In *Cathy's Curse* (1976), a little girl is also possessed by a demon which hides in her doll.

But make no mistake about it: in horror films it is often the children who are real little devils. Maybe it is because adults are afraid of children? You would really think so, because there are masses of films where adults (who always know best – at least they think they do) are plagued by evil children. In *The Child* (1977) one such evil child gets control over a group of zombies and sends them to attack the adults. In *Bloody Birthday* (1986) three children are without a soul because they were born during a solar eclipse, and they kill heaps of people. Something similar happens in *Devil Times Five* (1974), where five evil orphans escape and start murdering adults. In *The Godsend* (1980), an adopted child kills her foster siblings just so she can be alone. And in *Mickey* (1992) an angelic-looking boy turns out to be a heinous killer.

The children are not always to blame for their behaviour. In *Village of the Damned* (1960, remade in 1995), a number of children are born under the influence of an alien power, and they see humans as some kind of primitive animals. Their extraterrestrial powers allow them to burn people. In the sequel *Children of the Damned* (1964), the children even become symbols for universal peace, something the world is not ready for. The main characters of *The Children* (1980) are essentially innocent too. In the film, a busload of children gets infected by radioactive material and turn into zombies, setting fire to people by touching them with their hands.

Many of these films are a kind of warning to adults to take better care of their children. If you don't, you get children like the *Children of the Corn* (1984), who worship the "god of the corn" and kill everyone over the age of eighteen. Or you end up with someone like *Carrie* (1976, remade in 2013). Carrie is a normal girl, although a bit shy and lonely, who possesses enormous telekinetic powers (she can move objects with her mind), which she uses when people insult her. Many people die in the film, but it is not really Carrie's fault. All she ever wanted was to have friends and be popular.

Babies with sharp teeth

In horror films there are babies as well as children. I am deadly serious! In *Rosemary's Baby* (1968) Rosemary is expecting a baby, but the baby turns out to be a son of the Devil. It gets even worse in *It's Alive!* (1974), where unborn babies are exposed to radiation. When they are born, they come out as little monsters with sharp teeth, tearing humans to shreds. In *It Lives Again* (1978) and *Isle of the Alive* (1987), you can see how it ends for these monstrous babies. In *The Unborn* (1991) and *Creepozoids* (1987) too, you see babies who like nothing better than to sink their teeth into adults.

Little monsters

You don't have to be a baby to be a little monster in a horror film. The first film to show "little monsters" was *Don't Be Afraid of the Dark* (1973), where a group of small, human-like creatures hide in a chimney they drag people into. In *The Gate* (1987) and *The Gate 2* (1989) the little monsters come from outer space, but they are after the same thing: human flesh. The creatures in *Gremlins* (1984) and *Gremlins 2: The New Batch* (1990) are cute animals that turn into evil monsters when you feed them or give them water to drink. In *Ghoulies* (1984, plus three sequels: 1988, 1991, 1994), the monsters come out of the toilet bowl! In *Critters* (1986, plus three sequels: 1988, 1991, 1992) they come from outer space. They are furry, little round creatures with sharp teeth and red little eyes. Most of these films are meant to be funny rather than scary.

Human creeps

It is not just animals that can be monsters. Human madness has been the inspiration for many horror films too. The American actor Vincent Price played many such dangerous lunatics in horror films like *House of Usher* (1960) and *The Abominable Dr Phibes* (1971).

One of the most notorious human monsters is Norman Bates, played by Anthony Perkins in Alfred Hitchcock's *Psycho* (1960). Norman Bates dresses up as an old lady in order to kill people. The original film was followed by three sequels and a TV series.

In *Edge of Sanity* (1989) Anthony Perkins plays Jack the Ripper. Jack the Ripper was a man who murdered eight women with a knife in Victorian London and was never found. More than ten films were made about this mysterious serial killer.

There are many serial killers in horror films, such as Hannibal Lecter in *The Silence of the Lambs* (1991) and its three sequels (2001, 2002 and 2007). But the uncrowned king of film psychos has got to be Jack Torrance, played by Jack Nicholson in Stanley Kubrick's masterful psychological horror film *The Shining* (1980).

In the 1970s a new kind of horror films was born. They are known as "slasher films" or "splatter films". The story is almost always the same. Some lunatic or other escapes from a mental hospital and starts killing people, usually young and silly individuals. Once you have seen one, you have seen them all. They are all horrific and very gory, but they have nothing to do with the true art of horror.

Then *Nightmare on Elm Street* (1984) came out, which was followed by a whole series of films, video games, comics and a remake in 2010. Robert Englund (who had an excellent role in the TV series *V*) plays Freddy Krueger in the films and series. Krueger is a child murderer who is burnt alive by the parents whose children he kills. While his body dies, his soul lives on as he manages to enter the nightmares of a group of teenagers, luring them to their death. The *Nightmare on Elm Street* films are very well made, with good special effects. Freddy Krueger has become a very popular figure. He wears fashionable clothes and always tells bizarre jokes. There are even Freddy Krueger T-shirts, dolls and stickers.

Scary but fun

Freddy Krueger is typical of the modern horror film. He is a nasty figure who kills children. And yet he is popular with teenagers because he is weird as well as terrifying. In America there is a TV series about Freddy Krueger. These films are scary and fun at the same time. But they are not suitable for young children.

If you have the stomach for it, you should be able to feel your skin crawl and still continue to watch the rest of the film. And you should laugh, because that is what a horror film is all about. We want to watch it and feel the horror, but then we want to be able to go to bed and sleep peacefully and not have nightmares.

So I am warning you again: most horror films are not made for young children, but only for teenagers and adults.

9
Three Classic Horror Books

(by Jack Didden)

Over him hung a form which I cannot find words to describe
- gigantic in stature, yet uncouth and distorted in its propor-
tions. As he hung over the coffin, his face was concealed by
long locks of ragged hair; but one vast hand was extended,
in colour and apparent texture like that of a mummy... Never
did I behold a vision so horrible as his face, of such loath-
some yet appalling hideousness.

From *Frankenstein*, by Mary Shelley

Frankenstein

In the summer of 1816, four English travellers, three
men and a woman, stayed in a villa in Switzerland.
The weather was awful and the sky gloomy. A neverending rain was beating against the windows of
the Villa Diodati, where they were staying. The
dismal weather forced everyone to remain indoors.

The start of a horror story? Yes, but not like you imagine!

The four English travellers decided to light a fire in the library to get warm. Two of the men, Percy Bysshe Shelley and Lord Byron, were very famous poets. They rummaged around in the library and found a couple of books with ghost stories translated from German. One of them especially made a deep impression. It was called 'The History of the Inconstant Lover'. As a youngster, the poet Shelley had enjoyed scaring his sisters out of their wits with made-up vampire stories. The friends in the villa knew this, and suddenly Lord Byron had an idea: "Why don't we all write a ghost story?"

Easier said than done. Byron and Shelley soon had enough and went back to writing poems. The third man, a doctor called John Polidori, wrote a silly story about a woman who has to go through life with a

skull instead of a normal head. Initially, Shelley's wife, Mary Wollstonecraft, couldn't come up with anything. One night she was tossing and turning. That evening her husband and Byron had been talk-ing about the origin of life. "Maybe," Byron had said, "one day someone will discover how to create life." Mary couldn't stop thinking about this, and suddenly she had an idea for a story. She imagined a medical student who would try to create a living creature from the body parts of dead people. But the creature would turn out to be a monster. The student would panic and run away from his own creation.

This is the origin of the book *Frankenstein, or The Modern Prometheus* (Prometheus being a figure from Ancient Greek myths who made the first humans from clay). Mary wrote a short story about her vision, and her husband thought she should turn it into a book. Mary set to work, and two years later she published her novel.

The story is told by Captain Walton, an English explorer who is leading an expedition to the North Pole. As they sail through the ice, they see a man on a sledge. He is starving and nearly frozen to death. He comes on board, and when he has had something to eat and drink, he tells them his name is Viktor Frankenstein and begins his story. When he was studying chemistry in Ingolstadt, in Germany, he became obsessed with the question of how life started. He studied the human body and discovered how he could

create a living being. Once he had managed to make a living creature (he refuses flat out to tell anyone how he did it), it frightened him, because it was so hideous. He ran away, and when he returned to his laboratory the monster had gone.

After the monster's disappearance, Frankenstein has a nervous breakdown and takes nearly a year to recover. Then he has another shock. His young brother William is murdered by an unknown killer. Frankenstein returns to his family home and soon discovers that it is his monster who has killed William. He doesn't dare to tell anyone about it, and an innocent woman is found guilty and executed. One day, the monster visits Frankenstein and explains that he committed this horrendous murder because everyone hates him for his hideous looks. He blames his creator for this and, to take revenge on Frankenstein, he murdered the boy. His feelings of hatred will only disappear if he stops feeling so lonely. That is why he asks Frankenstein to make a wife for him. At first, Frankenstein agrees, but later he decides not to go ahead, because he doesn't want to be responsible for creating an entire race of monsters.

So after he has made a wife for the monster, he destroys her, and the monster gets very angry. In a rage, he kills Frankenstein's best friend, his wife and his father.

Frankenstein tries to hunt down the monster. This leads him to the Arctic, where he is eventually rescued by Captain Walton and his crew. In spite of the good care the captain takes of him, Frankenstein dies. Only moments after his death, the monster climbs on board and tells the captain that with Frankenstein's death his thirst for revenge has come to an end. "I shall die, and what I now feel be no longer felt." He jumps onto an ice floe and disappears into the darkness of the polar night.

The book was an immediate success, and it is still very popular to this day. It was the only bestseller Mary Shelley wrote. Her three other books were less successful. One of them, *The Last Man*, was a kind of science-fiction novel where the whole of the human race dies out because of a terrible epidemic, except for one man. This idea was used later by other writers like Stephen King in *The Stand* (1978), but no one reads Mary Shelley's original novel any more. Her name will always be connected to *Frankenstein*.

Dracula

That strange summer in Villa Diodati would lead to another classic horror book. As I mentioned before, John Polidori had come up with a silly story for the writing competition with his friends. He wasn't very happy with it either, and in 1819, a year after the publication of *Frankenstein*, he tried something else and wrote 'The Vampyre'. The story was published in a literary magazine without the author's consent, and was attributed to Byron. The story was in fact poorly written, but it is still a very important story, because it is the first one where a vampire is the main character. Two years after it came out, weighed down by depression and gambling debts, Polidori killed himself.

Despite Polidori's shortcomings as a writer, the story proved to be very popular, and the main character made quite an impression. It was the birth of a new fashion. Vampires became all the rage, and people couldn't get enough of them. In 1872 the first female vampire appeared in *Camilla* by the Irish writer Joseph Sheridan LeFanu. Almost thirty years after that, in 1897, the most famous of all vampire novels was published: *Dracula*, written by another Irishman, Bram Stoker.

Count Dracula looked just like the vampires that came before him. There was one crucial difference, though. Dracula was not English, but hailed from Transylvania in Romania. That made the story that much more exciting and mysterious. Bram Stoker had written four novels and a collection of fairy tales for children before that, but they were not very successful. Then he had a dream about a vampire. At least, that is what he later claimed. But what to call this vampire?

He came up with the name Dracula after he met a Hungarian professor called Arminius Vámbéry. They often had dinner together, and Stoker was fascinated by the stories his learned friend told him about a bloodthirsty Transylvanian prince who lived in the fifteenth century, Vlad Tepes, also known as

Dracula. Vámbéry returned to Hungary, but Stoker kept writing him letters full of questions about this fascinating fifteenth-century ruler. He thought that Transylvania, with its dense forests, would make a fantastic backdrop for a vampire story. Whatever the Hungarian professor didn't know or didn't tell him, he would look up in the library of the British Museum in London. He read all the books he could find on Dracula and studied all the maps of the region he could lay his hands on. Unfortunately, he made one mistake. In the novel, Dracula's castle is near the Borgo Pass. In reality it is near the river Arges, more to the east.

The novel is every bit as exciting as it was when it was first published one hundred and twenty years ago. The story is told through letters and fragments from diaries. A young Englishman, Jonathan Harker, travels to Dracula's castle because the count has bought a house in England. Jonathan works for a solicitor and is in charge of all the paperwork. He must also help the count with his move to England. Jonathan soon discovers his host is a vampire. He is locked up, but eventually manages to escape by climbing down the walls. But it is too late. Count Dracula has already gone to England. Together with nine coffins, he arrives by ship in the seaside town of Whitby in North Yorkshire. As chance would have it, Jonathan's fiancée Mina happens to be on holiday in Whitby, with her friend Lucy.

Lucy becomes Dracula's first victim in England. When she is dying, one of her friends, doctor Jack Seward, turns to his former teacher, Professor Abraham van Helsing for help. This Dutch professor discovers that Lucy was bitten by a vampire. He cannot save her life, but he manages to convince Seward, Quincey Morris (one of their friends) and Lucy's fiancé Arthur Holmwood that Lucy is now a vampire herself. That means there is only one way to "cure" her. With tears streaming down his face, her fiancé drives a stake through Lucy's heart and saves her from a miserable existence as a vampire. Then they start the hunt for Count Dracula, who is responsible for all this.

Next to Dracula's house in Whitby there is a mental hospital run by Jack Seward. One of his patients, Renfield, says he can "feel" Dracula's presence. One day, he escapes and shows Van Helsing where Dracula's house is. Seward and the others realize that a few coffins are missing. They start looking for them and discover they have been shipped to three different addresses in London. They visit these addresses and eventually confront Dracula. The vampire feels cornered and decides to go back to Transylvania. But in the meantime, Mina (now Jonathan's wife) has also been bitten. In her dreams she can see where Dracula is. That is how the others are able to cut him off before he reaches his castle. Just outside the castle a brief, violent fight takes place between the Englishmen and a band of gypsies, who are carrying Dracula's coffin. Quincey Morris manages to plunge a big knife into Dracula's heart, and the vampire turns to dust. Mina is saved in the nick of time, but Quincey dies of the wounds he received in the fight.

The real hero of the book is not Jonathan but the Dutch professor Abraham van Helsing, who knows all about vampires. It is no coincidence that he has the same name as the author (Bram being short for Abraham).

Almost everything we associate with vampires comes from *Dracula*. The fact that vampires can't stand mirrors (they have no reflection), the way they look, their hypnotic eyes, their fear of garlic and crucifixes, the fact that they can change into bats and wolves, and so on.

Dracula is the most important vampire novel ever written: a must for all true horror fans. In the twentieth century, a few writers have used Count Dracula as their main character. Two of the most interesting books are *Dracula Unbound* (1991) by Brian Aldiss and *Children of the Night* (1992) by Dan Simmons.

Dr Jekyll and Mr Hyde

The last book to become a true classic is Robert Louis Stevenson's *Strange Case of Dr Jekyll and Mr Hyde*. It was first published in 1886. In his short life (he died at the age of forty-four), Stevenson wrote many exciting novels. The most famous is *Treasure Island*, but *Dr Jekyll and Mr Hyde* also remains very popular.

Utterson, a London lawyer, hears the story of a man called Edward Hyde who severely mistreated a girl. The name rings a bell with Mr Utterson, and when he gets home, he digs up the last will and testament of Dr Jekyll, one of his clients. In it, he reads that after his death, or when he has been gone for more than three months, all his possessions should go to Mr Hyde. The lawyer is curious and starts an investigation. He asks one of Dr Jekyll's colleagues, a certain Dr Lanyon, for help, but he doesn't want to say much. Utterson suspects that the terrible Mr Hyde is blackmailing Dr Jekyll, but he cannot find any proof.

Then a certain Sir Danvers Carew is killed. It soon becomes clear that Mr Hyde was behind it. Utterson is very surprised when Dr Jekyll shows up with a letter in which Mr Hyde writes that he will disappear for good. But things get stranger still. Utterson realizes that Sir Danvers was killed with Dr Jekyll's walking stick. What is more, an expert claims that the handwriting of Dr Jekyll is the same as that of Mr Hyde. What is going on?

One evening, Dr Jekyll's butler comes to the lawyer's house to get him. His boss has not left his laboratory for a whole week. Utterson and the butler break down the door and find Mr Hyde's body next to a bottle of poison. Not a trace of Dr Jekyll. But they do find a whole load of papers. Meanwhile, Dr Lanyon has also died. He left a letter for Utterson that could only be opened after Jekyll's death.

From the papers and the letter, it becomes clear what happened. Utterson discovers that Jekyll was fascinated by the idea of what would happen if you allowed all your bad wishes to come out. He made a potion that would bring out all that was evil inside him. When he drank it, he became Mr Hyde, who was pure evil. But Mr Hyde became stronger and stronger. After a while, Dr Jekyll noticed that he would change into Mr Hyde even without drinking the potion. Because he didn't want to have any more crimes on his conscience, he killed himself by drinking poison.

The short novel – which was written in less than three days, according to the author's stepson – was a huge success. But the novel doesn't really fit with the other two I discussed in this chapter. The big difference between *Dr Jekyll and Mr Hyde* and the other two classics is that it doesn't have a true monster. Mr Hyde may remind us of Frankenstein's monster, but he is no other than Dr Jekyll, except that he looks different. Stevenson didn't mean to write a horror story. He wanted to remind people that we all have something evil inside of us – "man is not truly one, but truly two" as Dr Henry Jekyll says towards the end of the book. It is almost like a werewolf story in that respect. But because there have been a number of rather scary films based on *Jekyll and Hyde*, the book has become a sort of horror classic.

These three horror classics for adults were all written in the nineteenth century. That is not so surprising.

The Brits love a good mystery. That was even more so back then. People no longer felt very much at home in their rapidly changing world and became interested in things that were out of the ordinary. They were fascinated by the Middle Ages, old fairy tales and all things supernatural. In the nineteenth century people loved everything to do with vampires, ghosts, monsters and so on. In a way, things haven't really changed that much. Most horror stories are still written in English.

A highly successful children's author from the Netherlands, PAUL VAN LOON is best known in the English-speaking world for his *Alfie the Werewolf* series (published by Hodder in the UK). Originally an illustrator, Paul became a writer by accident when he could find no one to put into words a story he had thought of. He is never seen without his dark sunglasses, which has led to rumours that he is a vampire.

AXEL SCHEFFLER was born in Hamburg, Germany. He studied History of Art, before moving to the United Kingdom to study illustration at Bath Academy of Art in 1982. Since then he has worked as a freelance illustrator in London. He is best known for the children's books he has illustrated through his partnership with author Julia Donaldson. Together they created *The Gruffalo*, which has sold over five million copies in almost fifty countries throughout the world. He lives in London.

www.almaclassics.com